MARION FULLER ARCHER

There Is a Happy Land
Keys for Signe
Nine Lives of Moses on the Oregon Trail

Marion Fuller Archer

SARAH JANE

Albert Whitman & Company, Chicago

ISBN 0–8075–7241–1
Library of Congress Card Number 73–165816
© 1972 by Albert Whitman & Company
Published simultaneously in Canada by
George J. McLeod, Limited, Toronto
Printed in the U.S.A.

CONTENTS

SARAH JANE

 1 *Voyage's End*

THE STORM-BATTERED little steamship nosed into the dock. Wisconsin at last! The roar of the engine muttered away into silence. In the peace of that first silence in three days, Sarah Jane reached down and grasped Jonathan's hand firmly.

The immigrants crowding the deck were forgetful now of the discomfort of the stormy voyage along the Lake Michigan shore from Chicago. They pushed eagerly to set foot on their promised land.

Sarah Jane, too, longed for good, firm earth under her feet. She had had enough of ships to last her for her whole life. Six weeks on the sailing vessel from Liverpool to New York, three weeks more on the Hudson River and Erie Canal boats to Buffalo, and the long voyage across the lakes—Erie, Huron, and Michigan—which seemed to stretch endlessly from Buffalo to Chicago.

The quick change in Chicago to this coastwise steamer had given Sarah Jane no feeling of solid ground under her feet. And then had come the last three storm-tossed days. Sarah Jane was as water weary and hungry for land as the other passengers pushing around her.

In the crowd it would be easy, Sarah Jane feared, to lose a little four-year-old brother. She squeezed Jonathan's hand harder. The strain in his thin face melted into his puckish smile. It crooked his mouth and set one eyebrow up in a pert V. It put fiery points of light in the depths of his blue eyes.

"Why, Jonny! You smile just like Pa," Sarah Jane said, swinging his hand. The joy of remembering swept from her mind the lonely years in England without father or mother.

"Where is Pa? Let me see!" Jonathan clamored. The gaunt old Dutch woman against whom the crowd wedged the boy frowned at him. "Is this America?" he asked. "Where is my father?"

"Of course this is America, Jonny," Sarah Jane said. "It has been America since we got off the sailing ship in New York—remember? But this is Sheboygantown, in Wisconsin." Her tongue tripped over the strange new names she had been trying to learn properly since Pa's letter came three months ago. "As soon as the people ahead of us get off the boat, then we'll find Pa."

Jonathan bounced with glee. The old woman frowned at him again. Sarah Jane sighed, wishing people would not be so cross about a small boy's wiggles. But she remembered that the woman had been seasick all the way through the storm. Perhaps patience and kindliness would return when the woman was on firm land again.

Sarah Jane drew Jonathan nearer to her to prevent his annoying this fellow passenger. But this made Sarah Jane bump against the man in front of her.

"Now, stop dot bushing!" he scolded in his Dutch-accented English.

From behind, Sarah Jane heard Peg Cheney's voice. "Stop being a nuisance, you two children. Everyone's as anxious as you to get on land again."

"Yes, ma'am, Miss Cheney," Sarah Jane mumbled.

Peg Cheney was a friend of Matron at the orphanage where Sarah Jane and Jonathan had lived in the English city of Lincoln. Peg, too, was coming to Wisconsin, to live with her brother in a town named Fond du Lac. She had promised Matron to look after the children, to watch over their tickets and their food money, and at last to deliver them safely to their father, Edward Horner, in Sheboygan, Wisconsin.

Six stormy weeks the sailing vessel battled the waves of the Atlantic Ocean. Peg Cheney had groaned with every lurch and shudder of the ship. Other passengers overcame their seasickness, but Peg stayed in her berth, moaning and complaining, and Sarah Jane had to wait on her.

Sarah Jane thought many times that it would have been much easier to mind their tickets and food money herself. But Matron had been sure that a thirteen-year-old girl must be chaperoned across sea and land.

Four long years the Horner children had lived in Matron's orphanage. Parson Teller, from their church at home, had brought them to the orphanage for shelter after Mother and Grandmum had died in the same fearful, feverish night. Sarah Jane was nine then, and Jonathan a baby only four months old. There had been no other place for these homeless children.

"Mercy me," sighed Matron when at last it was time for them to leave. "I've watched you grow up, it seems like. I'll not be casting you out alone on the sea. Peg will see you safely to your father's arms."

Now they were in Wisconsin, and Peg's duty to them was finished.

As Sarah Jane inched her way along the deck toward her turn to walk down the gangplank, she recalled the April evening, more than four years ago, when Pa had left Stickney, their village in Lincolnshire.

"I'm off to build a better life for us. You'll see— America is full of promise for a man willing to work," he had said jauntily. And as he had embraced his wife tightly for a moment he had murmured words Sarah Jane had not understood then. "Please be patient. It'll be a lot better world for the new little one to grow up in —you'll see."

What brave promises were made to meet in America next summer! A man who was clever with his hands, as a weaver had to be, surely could find good work in the new land. None of the family ever doubted it. With little more than a few clothes and the cello he loved to play, Edward Horner set off to find riches England no longer offered.

Before Sarah Jane was accustomed to living without her father, and while she was still dazzled over her baby brother, the epidemic of chills-and-fever struck in the village. People old and young were sick and dying in every cottage in Stickney. There was no one who could take a little girl and her new brother.

Long, lonely months dragged by in the orphanage. Mingled with her loneliness for Mother and Pa and Grandmum, was Sarah Jane's homesickness for the little village. No one knew anyone else in the big city of Lincoln. The paving stones of the streets and the buildings huddled close together seemed to keep Sarah Jane a prisoner from the green grass and blue sky she had loved at Grandmum's in Stickney.

Then, one spring day, almost a year after Pa had left for America, Matron called Sarah Jane into her parlor. She held a letter from Edward Horner in America. She read part of it to Sarah Jane: "Times are hard here, too, but I will work and send for Sarah Jane and the babe as soon as I have saved enough money for their fare."

A wave of gratitude swept over Sarah Jane. "Pa does know about Jonathan," she thought. And Pa suddenly seemed real again, and closer to her than he had in months. But what was the matter with America? she wondered. Why couldn't Pa send the money right away?

So Sarah Jane scrubbed floors for Maggie the housekeeper. She dusted for Matron, she ran errands for Cook. Most important, she cared for little Jonathan. She wanted to make up to him for the loss of Mother. She sang in her funny, rough monotone the songs she made up about their angel mother in heaven and about their father in America, working to grow rich and build a fine home for them.

"You don't have a rich father. You're just a foundling and a pauper like the rest of us," Maudie jeered. Maudie's bed was next to Sarah Jane's in the dormitory, and most of the time she was Sarah Jane's best friend.

"Oh, yes, we do have a rich father in America," Sarah Jane argued. But the months dragged into years. Sarah Jane's back ached from carrying Jonathan. Her hands were chapped from scrubbing floors. Her stomach pinched with hunger because she put portions of her food on Jonathan's plate.

Sometimes Sarah Jane's courage ran low, and her memory almost failed as she tried to recall Pa's face.

Then, on May Day, 1852, Sarah Jane's thirteenth birthday, the letter came with the money for tickets and food and extra clothing. Sarah Jane was so happy that she never bothered to say, "I told you so!" to Maudie.

She kissed Maudie good-bye, almost ashamed of the joy in her heart as she saw the tears in Maudie's eyes. Poor Maudie had been dreaming for so long of being adopted into a real family.

Impulsively Sarah Jane put her only treasure into Maudie's hands. It was a tattered copy of Mr. Dickens's book *David Copperfield*. Parson Teller had brought it to Sarah Jane the last time he had come from Stickney to visit the Horner children.

"Here, Maudie, you may have this for your very own," Sarah Jane said. "Pa will buy me dozens of books in America."

Maudie held the book tight and promised, "Every word I read, I'll remember you, Sarah Jane. You are my best and only friend. Don't let the red Indians in America scalp you and kidnap Jonathan. I read a story like that in a book I borrowed from Cook."

Now Maudie and all the sadness, loneliness, and hard work at the orphanage were dimmed by distance. Inching along, Sarah Jane and Jonathan finally reached the gangplank. The years of being alone and poor would soon be ended.

Sarah Jane gripped Jonathan's hand. Her feet stumbled on the cleats in the gangplank as her eyes searched the dock for her father. She was looking for a well-dressed man like the prosperous-looking Americans whom she had admired in New York and Chicago. A richly dressed man with a crooked smile and puckish eyebrows like Jonathan's. And with a sudden rush of memory, she recalled how Pa's hair, golden like Jonny's, curled behind his ears and crinkled in a wave over his forehead.

But she could see no richly dressed, curly-haired, puckish-smiling American waiting on the wharf. Fear clutched her. What if Pa, too, were dead? It had been weeks since he mailed the money for their tickets.

Her fear made her steps falter. She stumbled and would have fallen if Peg Cheney had not caught her, saying, "Do watch your step, clumsy child!"

And then the voice which she had never forgotten called, "Sairy! Sairy Jane Horner!"

There was movement amidst a group of workmen standing near the end of the gangplank.

Jonathan broke away from her then. He ran to a smiling man who held out his arms. The man was so shabby that Sarah Jane had not given him a second glance in her search. Shabby, and bald, too, and with a face thin and lined. But truly, this man had Pa's blue eyes. And only Pa had ever said her name like that: Sairy.

15

But what had America done to Edward Horner, who had been so young and confident when he tramped down the sunset road toward Liverpool and the promise of America four years ago?

Then Sarah Jane, too, was smothered in the strength of his hug.

 ## 2 *Danger on*
the Plank Road

EDWARD HORNER drew his children aside from the crowd pushing off the boat. He thanked Peg Cheney for bringing his daughter and son to him. He gallantly refused to take the money left over from the cost of the voyage. Waiting, Sarah Jane was unable to check the tears streaming down her face. She dabbed the edge of her shawl against her eyes, but in a moment they were brimming again.

Some of the tears were tears of relief that never again would she be alone with the responsibility for Jonathan. Some were tears of grateful joy for the happy look on the little boy's face as his father held him nestled against his shoulder. Too often Jonathan had been a solemn little boy. Some were tears of sorrow that Mother could not be here to share this reunion. And partly, they were tears of happiness at being together at last.

She would look after Pa and Jonathan. She knew she could. Her busy mind pictured Pa wearing tidy, well-kept clothes, and Jonathan a tall, strong boy, well clothed and well fed, and all of them living in a neat, comfortable little home, kept by the capable hands of Sarah Jane.

She wiped her eyes again. There were tears of anxiety, too, at the great change she saw in Pa. There was a leanness, almost a gauntness about him, which frightened her. Lines in his sunburned face made her heart ache with the suspicion that America was not as welcoming and generous as they had thought it would be.

Peg's brother found her then. She hurried away with never another glance toward the children. Pa, still holding Jonathan, turned to Sarah Jane. He cupped her chin in his hand and turned her tear-streaked face toward him.

"Crying? Is that the way you greet your father after these long years?"

"I—I guess I always cry when—when I'm happy," she stammered.

"Well," Pa said, smiling at her, "I suppose there's crying that's mourning, and there's crying that's rejoicing . . . Sairy, you've changed so I'd hardly have known you."

"You've changed, too!" Sarah Jane's words rushed out, and she was glad they were said.

Edward Horner rubbed his hand over his bald head and then set his hat at a jaunty angle. "Yes, Sairy, you're right. It's time's arithmetic. The years that added inches to you have subtracted hair from my head while they divided our family." Sarah Jane laughed, and Pa winked at her before he went on. "But Jonathan here, I'd have known him anywhere without ever having laid eyes on him before."

"He is just like Mother, isn't he?" Sarah Jane said.

"The very image," Father agreed, sadness crossing his face. After a moment, he turned toward the street. "We should be starting. It's a long way home. Think you can travel two more days?"

Sarah Jane nodded, and he continued, "I left the

18

wagon and oxen over by the general store. It's too far for Jonny to walk and you to carry your things, Sairy. I'll load up the sack of meal and other staples and come back with the wagon to get you. It will take some time. Don't wander. There are plenty of sights to see right here. Mind now!"

Sarah Jane wanted to cry out "Take us with you!" but she trusted her father to know best and waved when he turned around to look at the children on the dock.

Jonathan's busy eyes had found something exciting on the lake shore. Tugging at Sarah Jane, he pointed to the crowd clustering around the freighter anchored near the little passenger ship in which they had come from Chicago.

"Look, Sar' Jane!" Jonathan exclaimed, as he pulled her along. He pointed toward the freighter.

On its deck was a locomotive. It was a small one, and a new one, Sarah Jane decided, judging from its shiny black paint. The locomotives she had seen in Liverpool and New York had frightened her because they always seemed about to blow up. This locomotive had no steam screaming from its pipes or its whistle, no smoke pouring from its bulging funnel of a smokestack, no fire gleaming orange in its black belly.

With much shouting and grunting and puffing and cursing, the men swarming around the locomotive unfastened blocks and cables that had held the locomotive on the deck of the freighter.

New ropes and chains and cables were fastened, then hitched to teams of powerful horses waiting on the shore. More tugging and grunting and shouting. Quick orders sung out to the horses. And slowly, slowly, the locomotive was hoisted up, swung over the water and set down on the shore.

Workmen swarmed around it, bawling at bystanders to get out of the way. Sarah Jane shrank back, but Jonathan, tugging her along, pushed his way to the very front line of watchers. He crowded close to the elbow of a workman who, with saw and hammer, had begun to fit wooden rims around the huge rear wheels of the locomotive.

"What you doin', mister?" Jonathan asked.

Sarah Jane blushed and tried to pull her brother back. But Jonathan paid no attention to her restraining hand.

"What you doin', mister?" he asked so insistently that the man paused to squint at him.

"What am I a-doin', sonny? I'm a-makin' felloes for to go around these engine wheels."

"Felloes? Felloes!" said Jonathan, singing out the syllables as he always did when he tried out the feeling of a new word. "What's felloes?"

"Felloes!" said the workman. "Well, sir, they are overshoes for this here train. What d'yuh think o' that?"

"Aw," Jonathan said, half disbelieving.

Sarah Jane ducked her head, wishing her brother would save his curiosity for less public places.

"Engines don't need overshoes," Jonathan said then.

The crowd of onlookers laughed, and Sarah Jane flushed.

The workman, glad for a chance to rest, filled a corncob pipe. He squatted beside Jonathan.

"This train needs overshoes," he explained amiably,

"but not for rain puddles like you do. This train has to wear overshoes to keep its wheels that are made for tracks from tearing up our new plank road."

"Why?" Jonathan asked.

Sarah Jane tugged at Jonathan, murmuring, "Don't bother the men, Jonny."

"Why?" Jonathan asked the man, ignoring Sarah Jane.

"Well you see, it's this-a-way," the man said, leaning his saw against the cowcatcher which fanned out ahead of the locomotive's front wheels. "Rock River Valley Railroad, way over yonder beyond Fond du Lac, has bought this engine. Made it out in the factory in Pennsylvania, they did, and shipped it clear out here. But it can't be all fired up and be chuffin' until it gets out to where the railroad is. So we are givin' the engine overshoes, me and my friend here, while the rest of us lay wooden rails along the plank road. Then a long string o' horses—ten, twenty, maybe forty of the strongest horses you ever did see—will pull this here engine over to the Rock River Valley."

"O-o-o-h!" said Jonathan, so awed that he was momentarily speechless. But then his roving eyes saw the word lettered on the side of the locomotive, below the window where the engine driver would sit.

"Look!" Jonathan cried, his voice shrill with excitement. "That's a big, big W. And there are two N's. I have two N's in my name, only not that way. And there's an A. I have an A, too. Why does it have all those letters?"

"I say there, you have lots of letters in your head for so little a sprout!" said the carpenter. "That's the locomotive's name—Winnebago. You can tell folks in years to come that you saw the Winnebago while she was still wearing overshoes."

Laughing at his own joke, the man picked up his saw and went to the other side of the locomotive. To Sarah Jane's relief, Pa appeared on the muddy road running along the dock. He was guiding a team of lean oxen hitched to a ramshackle wagon.

"Jonny, Pa is here," Sarah Jane said, firmly pulling her brother through the crowd.

"Meet Ned and Ted, come to pull you home," said Pa, hand resting on the bony shoulder of the near ox.

"I want to watch forty horses pull the engine!" Jonathan complained.

Edward Horner looked toward the locomotive at the water's edge. But he shook his head. He boosted Jonathan into the wagon, and helped Sarah Jane climb in beside her brother.

"It will be a day or two yet before the plank road has been fixed to take that engine," Pa explained. "And we need to get home to care for our pigs and cow and hens and all."

"Our pigs and cow and hens and all?" Jonathan asked excitedly. Overwhelmed to learn they had all those creatures, Jonathan forgot the locomotive for a moment. The oxen strained into their lumbering gait, and the wagon jolted down the road, with Edward Horner pacing beside the animals.

Then Jonathan remembered the locomotive. He squirmed to look behind them. But Sarah Jane pointed to a gaudy picture on the wall of the building they were approaching. It announced, "Coming Soon: Older and Company's Circus."

"Look, Jonny," Sarah Jane said. "There's a circus coming!"

"First circus ever to come to Sheboygan, so they tell me," Pa said, studying the picture as they neared it.

"Let me see the circus," Jonathan clamored, the locomotive forgotten.

"Next week Monday it's coming," Pa said. "By that time, we should be safe at home. Anyway, circuses cost a lot of money. They aren't for a poor man."

A shadow crossed his face, reminding Sarah Jane of hard, worrisome days when she was little. A poor man? Sarah Jane wondered. But he had come to America to be a poor man no longer. What had gone wrong?

Soon the family left behind the little town sprawled on the lakeshore and came to the plank road. Sarah Jane had once seen a boggy road in England mended with logs. But never before had she seen a whole road like this, plank after plank, the width of the road, on and on, until it disappeared in the green distance of trees.

As the afternoon wore on, she became aware of every plank as the wagon jolted across each joining. Not wanting to complain, she shifted uneasily on the narrow board seat of the wagon.

"Bumpity, mean old road," Jonathan complained.

"But it's a good road, Jonny," Sarah Jane said, wishing Pa had not heard him, "because it's the way home. And we can always walk with Pa if it gets too bumpy."

"Bumpy as this is, it's a great improvement over my first trip this way, in '48," Edward Horner said. "There was hardly a trail for us to travel. I got stuck in the mud every half mile, and we lost the better part of a day wandering off the trail. Lonesome as I was for you and your mamma then, I'd keep telling myself it's better they are safe in England until we have a smoother way here."

"But it would have been better," Sarah Jane said, "if we had come with you because we'd all have been together. We weren't really safe in England, Pa. Mother wasn't."

Edward Horner shook his head. "It's hard to tell, Sairy. This is terribly rough country for a delicate little think like your mamma."

Sarah Jane jumped down from the wagon to walk along the road beside her father. It was the strangest road she had ever seen. The eight-foot-wide plank road was bordered by a dirt road of equal width. This made it possible for wagons and carriages to meet and pass.

It was not hard for Sarah Jane to keep up with the oxen. They were thin and hungry looking. Other men, Sarah Jane noticed, had well-kept wagons and sleek plump oxen, but Edward Horner and his oxen shared the same lean, hungry look. It worried her, and worry was not what she had expected from this reunion.

At last, wilted by the heat of the sun and exhausted by the rough road, Sarah Jane returned to the wagon seat. She cuddled Jonathan and, with his head in her lap, he soon fell asleep.

It grew dark and heavy dew fell. Mosquitoes zinged from every puddle. Sarah Jane was relieved when a light shone ahead and Edward Horner guided the oxen off the road and into a fenced enclosure surrounding a log house.

He went to talk with a man and woman standing in the doorway, outlined by dim light behind them. Soon Pa returned with bread and milk and a bit of fried salt pork for supper.

When they had eaten, Pa helped Sarah Jane spread blankets on hay in the log barn behind the house. Hay for a bed? Sarah Jane was doubtful about it. It would prickle and tickle and keep her awake all night. But as her travel-weary body relaxed, she found that hay was the softest and sweetest of beds. She listened to Jonathan's quick breathing beside her and to her father's long, warbling snore. She smiled drowsily.

When she opened her eyes, it was morning. Jonathan was up, following Pa and asking questions without pausing for answers. They quickly ate the remains of last night's supper and set off for another day of jolting over the plank road. Edward Horner often had to pull the wagon aside to the bordering dirt road to let faster wagons rumble past.

By noon, the sticky heat was hard to bear. Relief came in midafternoon when clouds scudded across the sky, shielding the travelers from the sun. Jonathan was sleeping peacefully in the bed of the wagon. Sarah Jane jumped to the roadway to walk beside her father.

"Nobody ever told me it got so hot in America!" she sighed, wiping her forehead on her sleeve.

"Hist!" Her father held up a cautioning finger. Sarah Jane listened, too. There was a faint rumble of thunder.

"I wish we could have relief from the heat without danger of another storm," her father said. He sounded concerned.

At that moment a blue tongue of lightning split the

sky from top to bottom and the explosion of the thunder came almost at the instant of the flash. The oxen hesitated, tossing their heads.

"I think you'd better climb back into the wagon," Edward Horner said, halting the oxen. "When the rain comes, you'll have some protection up there, and you can keep a better eye on Jonathan. He'll be scared. I never heard a thunderstorm in England to equal those we have here."

Jonathan was sitting up, his eyes wide with fright. Sarah Jane crouched beside him murmuring words of reassurance which she did not honestly feel. Their father tapped the oxen into motion again and stepped back to walk beside the children.

"Up the road just a piece is the inn that Mr. Wade keeps for travelers, halfway 'twixt the shore and Fond du Lac," he explained. "Were we not so pinched for cash money I'd say let's stop there and have bite and bed. But meals and lodging for the three of us would cost seventy-five cents, and another seventy-five cents to stable the oxen —and I've not got that much."

"Oh," Sarah Jane said quickly, "we'd rather be alone with you than in an inn crowded with strangers."

"Sounds like your mamma—always accommodating and helpful," her father said. "It's a shame hard times keep us from stopping at the inn. Mr. Wade's inn seems like a palace in this wild country. They give you a royal welcome, folks tell me, and Mrs. Wade sets a tasty table."

Thunder had become a constant roar and rumble. Rain came, first large explosive drops, then a pelting downpour. Sarah Jane tried to shelter Jonathan with her shawl.

Wide eyed, he gripped his sister's hand. As the wagon reached the crest of a little hill, Sarah Jane saw ahead through the rain the inn her father had talked about. It looked white and bright against the inky sky.

The inn was a long, three-storied building. Wide verandas crossed the front on both first and second stories. Two wide doors opened invitingly at the front. Many windows, twelve-paned and trimly shuttered with black, gave promise of pleasant rooms inside. Long benches and rocking chairs lined the lower veranda.

Like most of the houses Sarah Jane had seen in America, the inn was a wooden building—a strange sight to her English eyes accustomed to stone houses and cottages with thatched roofs.

The inn stood on one side of the plank road, stables and barns on the other. Sarah Jane could see a man closing a stable door, but her attention was distracted by the noise of rushing water. The oxen were approaching a log bridge spanning a little river. Above the thunder, her father called, "Mullet River."

Before Sarah Jane could answer, a great halloo and a loud clatter of wheels sounded behind them on the plank road. Sarah Jane looked over her shoulder. Her heart skipped with fear. Speeding wildly toward them through the storm was a large carriage. Something was wrong, for the driver was standing, shouting and whipping his horses. His passenger, a veiled woman, clung to the frame of the carriage.

Sarah Jane clapped her hand over her mouth to stifle a scream. There seemed no place where Father could turn aside in time to let the speeding carriage gain the bridge.

As he tugged at the oxen, Sarah Jane bent over Jonathan to protect him against the collision she was sure would come.

By some miracle the carriage lurched past, so close Sarah Jane felt the whoosh of its speed. The oxen rolled their eyes wildly.

The carriage had barely passed when lightning struck nearby. The thunder was deafening. In terror, the oxen broke from Edward Horner's restraint and bolted forward. Heads tossing, tails high, they bellowed in fright, dragging the wagon crazily behind them. Everything in the wagon rolled and slid. The bundle of possessions Sarah Jane had brought from England flew over the side.

Sarah Jane held Jonathan tightly as the children were thrown from side to side in the wagon. In another flash of lightning she could see her father running after them.

The oxen plunged down the bank toward the rain-swollen river. The contents of the wagon were left strewed behind. In the rushing water, Ned stumbled and fell to his knees. Ted remained on his feet. The wagon tilted downward. There was a splintering sound. Water began to rise around the children.

"Sairy!" her father panted from the riverbank above them. Flat on the ground, he stretched both hands toward them. Sarah Jane boosted Jonathan up to him. She scrambled after him, up the tilting wagon box. The bearded man who had been closing the stable door ran toward them. He reached a hand to Sarah Jane. With a tug, he pulled her to the firm ground.

3 *Not To Be Beholden*

KEEPING A FIRM HAND on Sarah Jane's arm, the man turned to Edward Horner.

"Thank the Lord for a narrow escape!" he said.

Pa, who was holding Jonathan in a tight hug, nodded without a word.

"I'm Wade," the man went on. "Let's take the children over to my place. My wife Betsy and the girls will take care of them while you and I see what we can do about this wagon."

Already drenched to the skin by the heavy rain, and now oozing mud and river water with every step, Sarah Jane and Jonathan, hand in hand, followed Mr. Wade. He led them along the riverbank, across the log bridge, under the trees in the inn yard, and into the darkness of the pine and cedar fragrant woodshed at the back of the inn.

After explaining the mishap the children had just had, Mr. Wade left them with his daughter. "I'll bring your father along as soon as I can," he promised.

The young woman introduced herself, "I'm Polly Wade." She wrapped the shivering children in old shawls and continued, "We'll mop up the worst of this out here and then we'll bundle you up and you can sit in front of the cookstove in the summer kitchen. Mother will find some clothes to fit you."

"You—you are s-so k-kind," Sarah Jane said, trying to control the chattering of her teeth. "I'm Sarah Jane Horner, and this is Jonathan."

"You're not much smaller than my sister Ellen," Polly Wade observed. "And some of Hollis's outgrown things should fit your little brother." She patted Jonathan dry as she talked. Then she led them through a small pantry into the summer kitchen.

She set stools before the cookstove. Sarah Jane and Jonathan sat huddled in the shawls, grateful for warmth. Two boys peered at them a moment from a doorway beyond the stove. One of them was Sarah Jane's size. The other was half a head taller than Jonathan. Jonathan stared at them, but Sarah Jane clutched her shawl more closely around her. The boys darted back out of sight.

A kettle of something savory was simmering on the stove. Sarah Jane's mouth watered. At the back of the stove, behind the kettle, flatirons were heating. An ironing board, one edge resting on the table, the other on the back of a chair opposite the stove, showed Sarah Jane that this room was a busy part of the big inn.

Polly Wade returned, bringing bowls of bread and milk to the children.

"You are so good to us!" Sarah Jane said as she took the bowl Polly offered to her.

"Well, that's what we're here for, to help travelers on their way," Polly said cheerfully. "And you're more in need of help than many who pass by."

An older woman came into the room then with clothing over her arm.

"Mother," said Polly Wade. "This is another Sarah —Sarah Jane Horner."

"Pleased to know you," said Mrs. Wade.

For the flicker of a moment, the blue-gray eyes smiling through silver-rimmed spectacles reminded Sarah Jane of Mother. Her dark hair was frosted with gray, but it made an oval frame for her pretty face, as Mother's hair had always done. Mrs. Wade spoke, and the fleeting illusion was gone.

"I'm afraid you'll be thinking Wisconsin's not a very hospitable place!"

"With people like you, I'm thinking Wisconsin is the most hospitable place in the world," Sarah Jane said.

Mrs. Wade surveyed the bedraggled condition of the Horners. "Hot baths before anything else, Polly!" she said.

She turned to the room from which she had come, calling, "Sylvanus! Please get me the sitz bath. You'll find it in the back hall upstairs, I think. We'll set it up in the pantry, and they can bathe without bothering anyone."

Sylvanus, the boy who was Sarah Jane's size, came in a few moments with the sitz bath. Sarah Jane looked at it with interest. Painted black, edged with gold trimming, it was a small round tub, like a seatless chair with high scalloped back. Sylvanus placed it in the pantry, beside the long wooden sink. Polly filled the tub with hot water from the kettle steaming on the back of the stove. She tempered the water in the tub with cold water from the pump.

"Get your brother bathed and dressed," she suggested. "Then send him out, and we'll feed him some supper while you get yourself tidied up in these things of Ellen's."

Jonathan laughed when Sarah Jane lifted him into the elegant little tub. Food and warmth and friendliness had erased the terrors of the storm from his mind. Splashing and playing, he let her scrub with fewer complaints than usual. The outgrown clothing of the youngest Wade boy fit him perfectly. His fair hair, clean again, lay in damp curls around his face. Sarah Jane looked at him proudly for a moment. Then she said sternly, "Now mind your manners, Jonny!"

She opened the door and shoved Jonathan out into the summer kitchen. "Go find the nice lady," she whispered.

Then she returned to the luxury of her own bath. She washed her hair, pressed it as dry as she could and made a tight braid to hang down her back out of her way. She scrubbed away the grime of the hot journey and the caked mud from the riverbank which had dried on her legs.

While she was bathing, she heard men's voices. Her father and Mr. Wade had come. She put on the clothing of the girl, Ellen, whom she had not yet seen. The soft white underthings, edged with dainty lace, had a clean camphory smell about them. The dress was a pretty red calico with rows of little black leaves making an allover design. It had been mended at the underarm seams. Ellen had given it hard wear before it was packed away in camphor and lavender. Sarah Jane smoothed the dress admiringly. It was much prettier than the drab gray dresses Matron had chosen for her. When she was dressed, she tidied the room, mopping up the water Jonathan had spread.

She opened the door a crack and listened. The summer kitchen was dark and empty. Yellow lamplight shone from the room beyond. There was a strange whirr and stamp, the rattle of dishes, and suddenly Jonathan's laughter. Sarah Jane crossed the summer kitchen to the opposite door.

A girl who must be Ellen was clearing white plates and bowls and bone handled knives and spoons from a table beside the window. Across the room, Polly was mixing bread dough at the flour secretary. Near the door on Sarah Jane's left was a spinning wheel. The whirring noise came from it. Mrs. Wade was spinning. Jonathan sat on a three-legged stool, watching her.

"Here she is," said Mrs. Wade. "Fill her bowl with stew, Ellen. Your father and brother have already eaten, Sarah Jane, and now your father is out with Mr. Wade, getting things settled for the night."

Bowing shyly, Sarah Jane sat down before the bowl of stew.

"We'd better tell Sarah Jane all the plans for the night," Polly said. "By the time her father finishes his work, a heavy-eyed traveler like Sarah Jane should be upstairs in bed."

Sarah Jane looked up, startled. "We are going to make camp down the road a piece. It's no longer raining. There's no reason at all why we can't because Jonny and I are dry and clean, thanks to you. Father said that is what we were going to do—to make camp."

"Not tonight, dear," Mrs. Wade said, putting her

33

hand on Sarah Jane's shoulder. "Luckily we have one single room still unoccupied upstairs off the ballroom. We'll put you there. The dancers shouldn't stay too late tonight, and you'll be able to get a good night's rest before the drivers start stirring. Your brother is going to sleep with your father. We'll make up the buffalo robe bench in the taproom for them as soon as the Plank Road Association meeting is over. Jonathan is not very big, and I'm sure he can share the bed with your father."

"But—but didn't my father tell you?" Sarah Jane protested. "His cash money is all gone. We—we just can't afford to stay in your inn."

"An act of God in the shape of the storm and an impatient carriage driver stampeding your team hasn't left you much choice," Polly put in.

Sarah Jane looked questioningly at Mrs. Wade.

"You see," Mrs. Wade explained, "the right front wagon wheel was smashed and the axle is broken. So you can't drive on tonight. Your father is going to work in the smithy tomorrow with Mr. Wade, repairing the damages, and you'll be our guests tonight."

Tears suddenly stung in Sarah Jane's eyes. "You are the very, very kindest people I have ever known," she said huskily. "But we aren't beggars. We aren't charity children any more. That is why we came from England—not to be beholden."

"I understand how you feel," Mrs. Wade said. "And with all the work to be done around this house, there's no reason why anyone should have to feel beholden. You can help the girls and me tomorrow, and we shall be as adequately repaid as if your father had had the hard coins to lay on the counter. Would you be willing to do that, Sarah Jane?"

"Would you let me do that? Oh, I'd be so grateful," exclaimed Sarah Jane.

Mrs. Wade returned to her spinning. "Now you had better find your bed. Ellen will show you the way. Polly is going to put Jonathan to bed on the settee in the ladies' parlor until the plank road meeting is over and the buffalo robe chest can be made up in the taproom. Sleep well, my dear."

Carrying a small lamp, Ellen led Sarah Jane up the steep back stairs.

"Is it always so busy here?" Sarah Jane asked, as they stopped to catch their breath a moment in the second floor hall. Voices came from rooms up and down the hall. In the taproom below, men argued loudly. The beat of feet dancing to the music of a piano sounded from the ballroom over their heads.

"Sometimes a lot busier," Ellen said. "One day, over two hundred people wanted to stay here. Sylvanus and I kept a count—he made marks on the ground. But of course, with only twenty-seven rooms, we couldn't keep them all."

"But where do the others go who can't stay here?" Sarah Jane asked. "Do they camp, like Pa was going to do?"

"Some of them," Ellen said. "And of course some of them stop at the log tavern five miles west of us. But everybody would like to stay here. My mother is the best cook and hostess there ever was."

Sarah Jane nodded in emphatic agreement.

They went on up the stairs. A dance was ending. Laughing couples slowly left the dance floor to gather around a square piano at the end of the room. Ellen led the way around the ballroom which extended the full length of the inn's third floor. She took Sarah Jane to a corner room beyond, and opening the door, she went in and set the lamp on a table in the corner.

"Blow out the lamp when you are ready for bed," Ellen said. "Don't let the dancers bother you. They'll get tired soon. Later in the night, the coach and wagon drivers will come to the other rooms up here. Sam will be in the room next to you. He's fat and funny and noisy, but don't let him bother you. Here's one of my nightgowns. I'm a little taller, so don't start to walk in your sleep and trip and tumble."

The bed, gay with a patchwork quilt, filled one side of the room. With a table and chair, there was barely standing room for the two girls in the tiny bedroom. Sarah Jane patted the high bed, and it made a rustling, papery sound.

"What a soft, whispering kind of bed," she exclaimed.

Ellen laughed. "It has a cornhusk mattress. It'll whisper you to sleep. Have a good night. We'll call you in time for help with breakfast."

Quickly undressing, Sarah Jane hung her clothes on the hooks on the wall opposite the bed. She blew out the lamp. Then she climbed on the chair to look out the tiny three-paned window set close to the eaves. It overlooked the plank road. As she watched, men talking loudly came from the taproom. The meeting was over. Soon Father and Jonathan would be asleep in the buffalo robe chest.

What, she wondered, is a buffalo robe chest?

She climbed down, feeling suddenly forlorn. Not since Jonathan was born had she slept so far from him. She blinked rapidly. The misfortunes of the day suddenly raced through her mind and loneliness swept over her.

The cornhusk bed rustled noisily as Sarah Jane climbed into it, an odd bed in a strange land full of troubles. But as she relaxed in the high bed the sound of music from the ballroom reached her.

Listening intently, Sarah Jane concentrated. A scene from long ago took shape. Pa playing his cello in Grandmum's cottage. The music reminded her of that. Drowsily wondering if Pa still had his cello, she drifted off to sleep, comforted by the music.

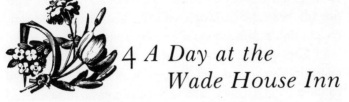# 4 *A Day at the Wade House Inn*

A STRANGE ASSORTMENT of noises roused Sarah Jane almost as soon as it was light next morning. In the other little rooms opening off the ballroom the coachmen groaned and stretched. Then they dropped boots and moved chairs and called to each other. Sarah Jane slid out of her whispering bed as quietly as she could.

After putting on her clean clothes from the bundle rescued from yesterday's mishap, she made her bed. Then she sat on her chair, wondering what she should do next. Carriages and ox-drawn wagons already rumbled along the plank road. From somewhere below her in the inn a bell tinkled. In a moment, there was a tap on her door. Sarah Jane opened it to a girl younger than Polly but older than Ellen.

"Good morning," the girl said. She looked at the bed already made and the tidied room. "There's nothing lazy about you, is there? I'm Sarah Wade. The lodgers are at breakfast now, and my mother thought you and your father and brother might enjoy eating together at the table in the kitchen."

Sarah Jane found her father and Jonathan waiting for her beside the family table with its cheery red-checked cloth and white dishes.

"I told you this is a hard and dangerous country," Edward Horner said as his family ate. "I'm sorry you have to learn it so soon and so roughly. But the country does seem to breed gentle and generous folk. Think what we owe to the Wades for their help!"

"Oh, but Pa," Sarah Jane said quickly, "I am going to help Mrs. Wade and Miss Polly all day, so we're not to be beholden."

"I know, Sairy," Edward Horner said. "Mrs. Wade has told me your plans and I'm grateful." He finished his porridge and tilted back in his chair. "But if it weren't for Mr. Wade and his kindness, I'm not sure how we'd get home with that smashed wagon wheel. He is a blacksmith as well as an innkeeper. He's going to repair the wagon in the smithy and shoe the oxen. I am indeed beholden to these good people."

With so much to think about, Sarah Jane quietly finished her breakfast.

Polly Wade appeared with a duster. "While the girls are clearing the dining room tables, you tidy up the ladies' parlor. Then dust the dining room before the first coach drives in for refreshments. After that, you and Ellen do the dishes. Then I'll be doing a washing, and you can give me a hand with the scrubbing."

Taking the duster, Sarah Jane went through the cheery dining room into the ladies' parlor. Jonathan followed her.

"Just peek at my bed—it's such a funny bed," he said, drawing her across the hall to the taproom, but he barred the doorway with wide stretched arms. "You're a lady. You can't come in here. Men only in here!"

Sarah Jane laughed at him. "Silly boy. It's a long time before you are a man." She peered into the taproom in the direction of his pointing finger. "Bed? What bed?"

All that she could see was a bench with broad seat and high back.

Jonathan laughed and pointed to the bench. "In it. In the buffalo robe bench. I slept there with Pa. It opens, and they put in a rustly mattress, and we slept there under the buffalo robe."

Sarah Jane returned to her dusting in the ladies' parlor. She paused beside the organ as she dusted it. Except that Jonathan was following her, she would have been tempted to pump the pedals and touch the keys. Reluctantly she left the pretty parlor and went to the dining room.

"Dust carefully around my mother's platters," Ellen said, pausing before the shelves between the dining room windows. "They're English, just like you are. Mother says they were made in Staffordshire. Do you know where that is? It's spatterware, and it's the peafowl pattern. Don't you think it's pretty? Wouldn't it be fun to eat off dishes like that all the time?"

"They are the most beautiful dishes I have ever seen," Sarah Jane said. She lifted her finger to stroke gently the blue spatter border of the platter. The design in the center showed a bright blue, green, and red peafowl roosting on twining vines. "They are too beautiful to be real."

"Oh, they're real all right," said Ellen. "Nothing unreal could cause so much work. They are my mother's wedding china. She brought them all the way from Pennsylvania in the covered wagon."

Sarah Jane finished dusting the dining room, but it was hard to keep her eyes from the peafowl dishes. Feeling bruised from just two days of jolting along in a wagon, she wondered how the delicate dishes could have survived a cross-country ride.

"Come on!" called Ellen. "There's a whole sink full of dishes for you and me."

As she followed Ellen through the summer kitchen, Sarah Jane found Jonathan perched on a high stool, industriously moving the dasher up and down in a churn.

He interrupted the wordless little song he was humming to say, "Look! I'm making butter for Mummy Wade. I'm helping, too. Nobody is beholden!"

Sarah Jane hugged Jonathan and smoothed his tousled hair.

When Ellen and Sarah Jane had finished the dishes, Polly called Sarah Jane into the backyard. She was bending over a steaming washtub.

"While I gather the bedsheets which are already dry for Sarah and Racheal to mangle," Polly suggsted, "you might scrub your things and Jonathan's to see if you can get the river mud out."

Mimicking Polly, Sarah Jane rolled up her sleeves. Polly showed her how to rub soft yellow soap on the long, narrow corrugated washboard which was then rubbed over the dirty clothing. Most of the dirt scrubbed away.

When the laundry was finished, Ellen led Sarah Jane to the garden patch. Together they dug a basket of potatoes. Then they carried a side of bacon from the little stone smokehouse at the bottom of the garden.

As Sarah Jane waited for Ellen to close the smokehouse door, she could hear the ringing blows of hammer on anvil in the nearby smithy.

"Let's watch for a moment," Ellen suggested, joining Hollis and Sylvanus.

Sarah Jane stood in the doorway of the smithy, out of reach of the fierce heat of the fire on the forge. When her eyes were accustomed to the glare, she saw that her father was working the bellows for Mr. Wade.

"Now they are going to shoe your old ox," Sylvanus explained. "Let's wait. Oxen are always funny to watch."

"Just for a minute," warned Ellen. "Mother needs these potatoes and bacon."

Andrew, the eldest Wade son, already a young man, led in old Ted. Sarah Jane watched in amazement as they fastened a sling around his belly and hoisted him up so that he dangled, helplessly bawling, while Mr. Wade replaced his worn shoes.

"Why do they do that to him?" Sarah Jane asked.

"It's because oxen are such clumsy old critters," little Hollis told her. "They can't stand on three legs to be shod, like horses do."

As Ted was lowered to the ground, Sarah Jane and Ellen turned back toward the inn, where they were busy in the kitchen the rest of the day.

The girls rolled pie crust for Mrs. Wade; they cut cookies for Polly. They scraped new potatoes and carrots, they shelled peas still warm from the sun, and no one scolded if they nibbled a sweet pea.

Ellen was so full of chatter that Sarah Jane had no time to think about her father's troubles or the problems her new home might bring.

When supper had been eaten and Sarah Jane had helped Ellen dry the snow-white ironstone dishes, Edward Horner called her to the innyard. The oxen were yoked and hitched to the repaired wagon. The Wades gathered round, as Edward Horner helped Sarah Jane to the seat beside Jonathan.

"It's so late, it seems a pity to see you start out now," said Mrs. Wade. "Sarah Jane has worked enough today to pay for three nights' lodgings for all of you."

Edward Horner bowed. "We are grateful to you for your kindness. But there is a full moon tonight and we should be able to travel quite a piece before we have to make camp. I've been away longer than I had expected. It's like I told you. My wife is—is not strong just now. I must be getting home."

Mrs. Wade kissed Sarah Jane then, and there were cries of farewell as the Horners started on their way.

Mechanically Sarah Jane waved until she could no longer see the Wades. Then she sat hunched on the wagon seat, trying to believe she had not heard what Pa had said.

"My wife," those were his words. Why had he not told her before?

The sun went down, but the full moon lighted the plank road. Jonathan fell asleep with his head on Sarah Jane's lap. She sat stiffly. It was as if something had turned to stone within her at the words her father had spoken to Mrs. Wade.

 ## 5 *The Intruder*

ON AND ON through the early night hours the oxen plodded. The wagon jolted over the planks. Edward Horner walked beside the team. With troubled eyes he looked back at Sarah Jane's withdrawn face. He did not speak, and she did not speak. She felt too hurt, angry, and betrayed.

The moon dropped out of sight behind the trees in the west, and Edward Horner directed the oxen off the road to an opening beside a little brook.

"I hate to drive you so long, Sairy dear," he said quietly, for Jonathan still slept in her lap. "You worked hard all day. But I can't be away from home any longer. Now we'll rest for a few hours and eat the food Mrs. Wade packed. We'll go through Fond du Lac tomorrow and be home by evening."

He laid his hand over Sarah Jane's, but she quickly pulled it away from him.

"Sairy, Sairy!" he said. He reached out as if he would take her hand again. Then he dropped both hands to his sides. "I'm sorry you heard about Rebecca that way. I should have told you before, but the right time didn't seem to come. I've been deliberating how best to tell you. I didn't write it in the letter, because I thought it would have looked stark and somehow unloving just put down flat on paper. And it is really the most loving thing that could happen to me or you—and especially to little Jonathan. He needs a mother, Sairy."

"He has a mother in heaven," Sarah Jane said, swallowing a sob.

"The loveliest mother in God's world," Edward Horner said. "But Sairy, a mother in heaven can't take care of a little boy down here on earth. Rebecca has a loving heart just waiting for a little boy to love. Her own little boy died so young. He was born on the ship coming over here. And she had to bury him, along with her little girl, in the middle of the ocean. Ship fever took them both."

He paused to unyoke the oxen and tether them where they could browse in tall grass. Sarah Jane sat biting her lip to keep from sobbing. Her father returned to stand beside her.

"Rebecca's waiting to love you and Jonathan and care for you as tenderly as she has cared for me. She saved my life when I had cholera in '50."

"Mother loved you!" Sarah Jane said accusingly, keeping her hands tightly clasped.

"And I love your mother," he said, emphasizing the present tense. "Just as Rebecca loves her husband, David, who was killed in a mine accident in Wales just before she came to America."

A sob shook Sarah Jane's shoulders. She drew her shawl across her face. Her father patted her arm. His breathing sounded heavy in the darkness, as if he, too, battled a sob. Then he spoke again.

"Love is not a weak, short-lived thing, Sairy. It doesn't lose its power when the one you love is gone. I'll never stop loving your mother. And I know Rebecca will always love David in that special way I love Jane. But in this rough land, a woman needs a husband; a man needs a wife. Why, just think, Sairy, I couldn't stay in from the fields to care for Jonathan, and he's still a little boy."

"But I am here to care for him," Sarah Jane said heatedly. "I have taken care of him all his life."

"And well, too. But you are still a girl, my dear. These years without your mother and me haven't given you enough time for girl things. Now you must go to school, you must play and be joyful. You must learn to be young and happy, too, or you'll not be ready to live wisely when you grow up. A person needs to be strong in this new land, and you are strong. But most of all, a person needs a fountain of joy inside to face life here. Can't you see that it's best for all of us, having Rebecca?"

Stubbornly Sarah Jane shook her head. "I wish you hadn't ever sent for us. Why didn't you leave us in England?" She was crying now.

"And leave you and Jonathan in a charity children's home? Sairy, I love you too deeply for that."

"Pa, let me go back to Wade's," Sarah Jane said suddenly. "I can't go where someone is stealing Mother's place. I'll work for my keep at the Wades. You take Jonathan and go on. I—I can't."

"Sarah Jane!" Her father was stern. "You are coming with us. Rebecca is not stealing your mother's place. She is in her own place, in my heart and in our home.

You are coming with us for the very reason you started from England in the first place. Because we need each other. You need your father and you need the mother's guidance a wise and loving woman like Rebecca can give you. Jonathan needs a family. So do you, Sarah Jane."

Sarah Jane shook her head. "I suppose—I'll go with you—until—" Her voice trailed away. The turmoil within her was almost more than she could bear. Fathers were not to be disobeyed, but neither were mothers to be dishonored. Her father paced up and down the length of the wagon.

At last, with a sigh he said, "Come, now. We must both sleep or we'll be too tired to press on home before dark tomorrow."

Sarah Jane could not sleep, she could not cry. While Jonathan and her father slept, she stared at the stars slowly moving down the sky and she saw dawn brighten the clearing. A stepmother! She had never anticipated such a possibility.

Later, Sarah Jane had little memory of the next day except for its misery. She felt she must have passed the day staring straight ahead.

They reached the village called Fond du Lac. For a moment, Sarah Jane wondered if she could find Peg Cheney and work for her. But they left the plank road to skirt the shore of Lake Winnebago, sparkling and blue in the summer sun.

None of Sarah Jane's depression reached Jonathan to dampen his delight in his father's companionship. Often throughout the day Edward Horner talked to Jonathan about the new mother he would find in their little log cabin home. There would be cousins, too, in the Welsh settlement. Jonathan clapped his hands.

"A real mother to rock me and sing to me and love me," Jonathan said, and Sarah Jane felt a jealous pang. She turned her shoulder to her father and Jonathan and cried quietly. Never had she thought Pa would betray them.

When Jonathan settled for a nap in the back of the wagon, she spoke to her father. "When—when did you— did you marry this Rebecca?"

"Last summer," he answered. "In May of '51. When I fell sick of the cholera the year before, her brother took me to his house, over in the Welsh settlement. Rebecca nursed me back to health. Many a man and woman and child no sicker than I was died during those awful days of the cholera, Sairy. We owe Rebecca much."

As she watched her father plodding wearily along beside the wagon she was ashamed of her anger. But she felt nothing could wipe away the hurt of knowing that someone else was in Mother's place, robbing Sarah Jane of her right to care for Pa and Jonathan.

"There's one more thing I should tell you now," her father said later. "Your stepmother speaks mostly Welsh. And of course I don't speak any more Welsh than she does English. But there's a language of love that bridges all other tongues and somehow I've never felt the lack of speech until now. Our farm isn't far from the Welsh settlement—if we need an interpreter, Rebecca's brother comes over and helps us out. But as I said, there's a language of love that goes beyond words. So we don't have to appeal to Thomas very often. It may be different now that you and Jonathan are here. You'll need to talk to get acquainted."

Sarah Jane wanted to protest that she never wished to get acquainted, but she was afraid of the stubborn lift to her father's chin. The warmth in his eyes and the love in his voice when he spoke of Rebecca checked Sarah Jane's tongue.

Toward evening, Edward Horner stopped the oxen at the top of a little hill. Below was a clearing: a small field of grain, a garden plot, a log barn and a shed, and at the center of the clearing, a log house. The open door was flanked on each side by a small window. Smoke rose from the chimney at the end of the cabin.

"Home!" exclaimed Edward Horner. "Not a mansion like Wade House, Sairy, but it is ours and it's home."

As he spoke, a woman came out of the door, waved, and walked rapidly toward them. Edward Horner clucked to the oxen and they moved forward. Sarah Jane closed her eyes. "If she looks like Mother," she told herself, "I don't think I can stand it."

Edward Horner hurried ahead to Rebecca. Sarah Jane closed her eyes again as Rebecca ran into Edward's arms. The oxen went on unguided until they reached the man and woman standing in the road, then they stopped. Jonathan scrambled eagerly out of the wagon. His father caught him up, and in another moment Jonathan was in Rebecca's arms, his cheek against hers.

Reluctantly Sarah Jane rose. She took her father's hand and dismounted from the wagon. She avoided the challenge in his eyes, then she faced her stepmother.

Rebecca was tall, almost as tall as her husband, and

strongly built. What had Pa meant when he told Mrs. Wade, "My wife isn't strong now"?

Rebecca was dark-skinned, her hair was blue-black, her eyes were brown, and her face was angular and strong. in every way, she was the opposite of Jane Horner, who had been tiny of body, blond of hair, with white skin and blue eyes in a soft, round face. For a moment, jealousy stung Sarah Jane. Was Rebecca's very difference an insult to Mother?

With a slight hesitation, Rebecca put Jonathan down and held out both hands to Sarah Jane as if she would have embraced her, too.

"Sarah Jane!" She said it musically, with a burring of the R and a strange foreign lilt.

Ignoring the offer of an embrace, Sarah Jane stiffly shook hands with her stepmother.

The tense moment was broken when Edward Horner spoke to the oxen, linked one arm through Rebecca's and the other through Sarah Jane's. Thus, with Jonathan skipping ahead, they walked toward the barn.

Speaking slowly, Edward Horner explained the accident to Rebecca and the day spent repairing damages at the Wades. Rebecca followed his words closely, concern on her face.

"Do you understand, Rebecca?" her husband asked.

"I—under—stand," she said haltingly.

She understands better than she can speak, Sarah Jane thought. And for a moment she felt pity for her new stepmother, having to hear an unknown tongue even in her own home. And watching her, Sarah Jane admitted to herself, "She's beautiful, and I wish she weren't!" This homecoming she had been looking forward to for so long as the end to problems was so different from her expectations.

Rebecca led the way into the log house. It was plain and bare, compared with the luxurious Wade House, but it was clean and neat. The floor of unevenly worn white wood was scrubbed spotless. Opposite the door was a table set with four places. At one end of the room was the fireplace. On a crane extending over it was an iron pot with something bubbling that gave forth a fragrance which made Sarah Jane's mouth water and her stomach contract with hunger.

Across the length of the room opposite the fireplace a curtain partly concealed a bed. A roomy black rocker was pulled cozily in front of the fireplace.

Interrupting Sarah Jane's examination of the room, Rebecca took Jonathan by the hand and led him to a little shelf pegged into the wall. "Look," she said, and it sounded like a song, not a word. "Look, little Jonathan—your mother."

With a cry, Sarah Jane ran across the room to see. It was the little tintype portrait of Mother which Pa had carried to America with him. Sarah Jane turned to her father who stood behind her.

"Rebecca had me build the shelf for it," he explained. "She says you and Jonathan must never forget your mother's face."

Unable to say anything, Sarah Jane bent forward toward the little portrait. She took it from the shelf and held it so that Jonathan could see it more plainly. After a moment, Rebecca led them to the supper table.

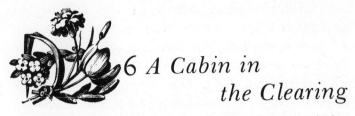

6 A Cabin in
the Clearing

JONATHAN FELL ASLEEP, his head on the table, before
the family had finished plates filled with chicken and
dumplings. Rebecca took him gently in her arms and
undressed him without rousing him. As she washed his
face, still smudged with the dust of the day's travel, he
stirred. She sang softly a moment, and he was asleep
again when she tucked him into the trundle bed pulled
out from under the big bed.

Sarah Jane watched, amazed. All Jonathan's life bedtime had been a prolonged struggle for Sarah Jane.

"Now, Sairy, I'll show you your bed," her father
said. Taking the bundle which had come with them from
England, he led her to a ladder nailed to the wall beside
the fireplace. She followed him up through a hole in the
ceiling.

The attic room was bare and rough. It was still hot
even though long, narrow windows in each end of the
cabin were open. A bed, not very wide, was built into the
wall. Above it was a shelf with a candle. There were
pegs on the opposite wall for holding her clothes. Although rough, and stifling now with heat, it was a room
of her own. Sarah Jane was grateful.

"Th-thank you, Pa. It—it is a very nice room for me," she said. "I'm so tired, I think I'll go to bed right now, please."

"But you must say good night to your stepmother," he chided her.

"Pa—" she faltered. At this moment she did not think she could face this stranger.

Below them, Rebecca spoke, "Enough now, Edward!"

He hesitated a moment—an uneasy moment for Sarah Jane because she dreaded being scolded for her unfriendliness. But he turned and descended the ladder.

Sarah Jane undressed and put on her nightgown. She went to the eastern gable. Sitting on the floor beside the window, she looked out at the stars beginning to prick the twilight sky.

She was exhausted by fatigue and her own emotions. She had expected joy at being free of the adult responsibility she had felt for Jonathan. She had daydreamed of a home in America for her father, her brother, and herself. A fourth person had never occurred to her.

A day ago, when she had first learned of Rebecca's place in the family, she had resolved never to accept her. But the real Rebecca, even in this short time, made it difficult for Sarah Jane to dislike her. How gently she had put Jonathan to bed! Sarah Jane dropped her head on the window ledge and cried.

Her father and stepmother were talking on the doorstep below, a strange, one-sided conversation. Her father spoke slowly and distinctly and at great length. Rebecca answered in single words or short phrases.

What an unusual life to lead, with a wife to whom

you could not talk, Sarah Jane thought. Why, *why* had Pa done it?

After a long time, the voices were still. Sarah Jane heard then the rustling of a cornhusk mattress, and a long, tired sigh from her father. Then, she saw movement in the shadows below her. Rebecca walked in the moonlit yard to the little springhouse. When she came out and fastened the springhouse door, she was carrying a cup and had a towel over her arm. She entered the house. Sarah Jane put her head down on her arm, wondering what life would be like with this stepmother to whom she could not talk.

Steps sounded on the ladder. Rebecca tiptoed into the attic and crossed the little room. She bent over Sarah Jane, gently touching the girl's hot forehead. She used words Sarah Jane could not understand, but her tone was tender and sympathetic.

Kneeling, Rebecca bathed Sarah Jane's hot face with the towel dipped in cool water. Then she offered Sarah Jane the cup from the springhouse.

"Drink, Sarah Jane," Rebecca said.

Taking the cup from her stepmother, she drank the cool milk gratefully. Then Rebecca drew Sarah Jane to her feet and led her to the bed. "Now . . . Sarah Jane . . . sleep," she said softly.

Obediently, Sarah Jane lay down on her bed. She marveled at how much meaning Rebecca could put in a few words. She strained her eyes, trying to read the expression on Rebecca's face, but the light of the moon did not reach this corner. She wondered if her stepmother would try to kiss her good night. Should she turn her face away?

Rebecca bent and bathed Sarah Jane's face, damp again with perspiration in the heat of the attic. Softly she said, "Good night, dear." Then she turned and went down the ladder.

Sarah Jane was grateful that she had not had to turn her face away from her stepmother's kiss. Drowsily she thought of how long it had been since she had been tucked into bed at night.

Sunlight in the eastern gable window finally awoke Sarah Jane next morning. The room below was quiet, but somewhere outside she could hear Jonathan's chatter. It must be midmorning! After dressing, Sarah Jane backed down the ladder.

The trundle bed was out of sight, the big bed was made up, and the table was cleared. Sarah Jane stepped to the open door. Far across the clearing, her father worked in a field. Jonathan, squatting in the rows of a tidy garden near the door, was pulling weeds, holding each one up to ask, "Is this right, Mummy?"

Sarah Jane cringed. Resentment burned in her again, but she paused, trying to control herself.

Rebecca, sitting in the shade of a big tree, was darning the ragged knees of the shabby little knickers Jonathan had worn in the orphanage. Folded on her lap was Sarah Jane's second gray dress, the worn spot under the arm neatly mended.

As Sarah Jane hesitated in the doorway, Rebecca looked up from her sewing. Seeing Sarah Jane, she smiled and rose, calling, "Edward, come!"

Morning teatime was plainly a ritual Rebecca loved. When she had stirred up the fire and swung the teakettle over the flames, she sliced bread, set out a patty of butter and a bit of honeycomb. The family sat around the table. Tea steamed in their cups. Jonathan had a bowl of bread and milk. Rebecca said in Welsh a short prayer to which Edward Horner added "Amen."

While Sarah Jane slowly sipped her tea and ate her bread and butter, a nibble at a time to postpone talk, her father ate quickly, pausing between bites to voice his worries about the farm. That, at least, was as she remembered it in England: her father quarreling with the land. To weave firm, beautiful cloth at his loom, to play lovely music on the cello—those things Edward Horner could do with his long, strong fingers. But he was not a good farmer. Even as a tiny girl, Sarah Jane had shared that knowledge with Mother and Grandmum.

Her father drained his cup and set it down forcefully for emphasis. Then he looked at Rebecca who shook her head slightly. His words had been too rapid and angry for her. Impatiently he took his refilled cup from Rebecca. He lifted his voice, as if loud speech would be easier for her to understand.

"The corn—it was not a good crop to begin with, and that storm while I was away beat more than half of it down. Hail—you must have had hail around here. Hail?"

His voice was almost a shout as he finished. Jonathan looked up, his face puckered with distress. For a moment Sarah Jane was ashamed of her father. After all, it was not his wife's fault that she did not understand his language, any more than it was his fault that he did not speak Welsh.

Rebecca stood and gathered the tea things. "Hail—

yes," she said. She hesitated as if she wanted to say more, but she turned away with a shrug. Pa had not changed, Sarah Jane realized. A long repressed memory came back. His fuming used to bring that same shrug to her mother's shoulders.

Sarah Jane held her breath, hoping for cheerful words from her father to break this distressing moment. But none was spoken.

"Come, Jonny," Sarah Jane said to break the tension. "Show me what you were doing."

Jonathan took her hand, pulling her to the garden. "There's a garden for weeding," he explained. "And now here's a cow for milk. Look. Isn't he big?"

"She," Sarah Jane corrected Jonathan, as she stood safely back from the fence. The cow looked rough and angular, like so much of this country. With short horns and short ears, and tail much shorter than the tails of English cows, she seemed almost another kind of animal. The chickens that clucked nearby looked more familiar.

Jonathan led Sarah Jane to a fenced enclosure on the other side of the barn. "Look, our pigs!" he said proudly as if he were the lord of the manor. "A mother pig and her six little pigs. By winter they'll be grown up, too, Pa says."

"Pigs?" Sarah Jane asked uncertainly. She backed away as the animals came pushing and standing on their hind legs, squealing and grunting, to the fence, eager to be fed. That they were pigs she could tell by their language of squeal and grunt, but they looked like very distant cousins of the round pink short-legged pigs which Grandmum had kept at the bottom of the garden in Lincolnshire.

These were gray and rangy long-legged creatures with short curly tails and determined looking snouts.

Jonathan showed her the cornfield damaged by hail. And beyond it he told her, pulling her along, "Look! Pa's flax—Pa's cash crop." She smiled to hear him echo his father.

Woods, dark and frightening to Sarah Jane, grew close to the field of flax. Words of warning about red Indians lurking in the forest flashed through her thoughts. She led Jonathan back toward the house.

When the children reached the cabin, Rebecca and Edward Horner were talking to a tall dark man so very much like Rebecca that Sarah Jane knew he must be Rebecca's brother, Thomas. And beside him was a girl, tall and dark, with glossy black hair and big smiling brown eyes. She looked enough like Rebecca to be her daughter.

Sarah Jane stood back shyly, but Jonathan ran to his father and leaned affectionately against him. Edward Horner, putting one hand on Jonathan's head, held out the other hand to Sarah Jane.

"Come speak to Thomas Hughes, Sarah Jane," her father said. "This is Rebecca's brother, and here is Eliza, his daughter, come to invite you to go to school with her when the summer term starts down at the brick schoolhouse."

Thomas Hughes bowed courteously and shook Sarah Jane's hand. Eliza smiled and nodded.

"A girl can't come too soon to her books," Thomas Hughes said. "Rebecca knows how often our father said to us, 'Goreau cof cof llyfr.' That means, 'A book has the best memory.' I'm thinking that while you learn from Miss Tillie Wallace all the memories her books have to give you, you can then be the teacher to this sister of mine. It's hard when a wife can't speak to her husband and a mother can't speak to her children."

He sounded a bit fierce as he finished, glancing at Rebecca. "Will you help us, lass?" he asked kindly as he turned to Sarah Jane.

"I—I'll do my best," she stammered.

"Good, good!" he exclaimed heartily. "I'll tell Miss Wallace you will be coming with Eliza Monday after next when school starts."

He turned then to boost Eliza to the back of the horse tied to the gatepost. He prepared to mount, too, but Rebecca stopped him with a rush of Welsh words.

Thomas Hughes turned toward his brother-in-law to translate Rebecca's request. "You'll need to make a trip to Oshkosh, Ed, for shoes that won't cripple the lass's feet."

Edward thought for a moment. "Yes, I can leave the corn tomorrow. We'll have the girl ready for school."

"Good!" said Thomas Hughes. "I'll tell Miss Wallace she has another scholar. And before long I expect my sister to be conversing in the tongue of the land."

He repeated his speech forcefully in Welsh to Rebecca. Then with a salute, he mounted the horse, and they trotted down the lane. Eliza turned to wave to Sarah Jane.

7 To Oshkosh

CHICKENS SQUAWKING and cackling awakened Sarah Jane at dawn the next morning. She leaped from bed and ran to the window. Robbers! That was her first thought. But it was her father who stood in the hen yard. He rushed at a hen, grabbed at it, missed, and almost fell. His clumsiness set the whole flock in an uproar.

Rebecca, who had been watching outside the pen, called her husband to her. He came out, mopping his forehead.

Poor Pa! Sarah Jane thought, he was never meant to be a farmer. When she was a small girl, they had lived in Nottingham where Pa was a weaver in a big mill. But machine looms had put hand weavers out of work, and with no work for Pa, there was no money to pay for food or a home. The Horners had set out along the wintry road to Stickney to share Grandmum's cottage.

Sarah Jane, a tiny lass then, rode on Pa's shoulder most of the way. Boys sometimes laughed at them in villages through which they passed, and they must have been a funny sight, Sarah Jane remembered. One slight man with a little girl clinging to one shoulder and a big cello bouncing along, balanced over the other shoulder. Wherever Pa went, his cello went, too.

Leaning out the window to watch Pa in the hen yard, Sarah Jane thought of those long ago days at Grandmum's. She was a widow, and Pa could be a help to her with garden and animals now that there was no weaving for his clever hands to do. But he had upset Grandmum's hens, too, Sarah Jane recalled, and set them squawking every time he went near them.

With a sigh at all the forlorn memories, Sarah Jane finished dressing while chickens squawked outside. She went to the window again. Rebecca stood with a struggling hen in each hand. She gave them to her husband.

"I do declare, Becky," he said. "You have a way with everything that moves and breathes. You put me to shame. Try for another good plump one. Three fat hens should bring Sairy a pair of school shoes, wouldn't you say?"

Before he finished speaking, Rebecca had caught another chicken.

Sarah Jane hurried down the ladder. Rebecca and Pa were coming into the cabin as Sarah Jane's feet touched the floor.

"I'm glad you're up," her father said. "You and I must get an early start for Oshkosh. Get your brother up and set out breakfast for us so your mamma and I can get eggs and vegetables and a bit of honey packed for trading."

Sarah Jane started toward the trundle bed to rouse Jonathan, but suddenly her father's words were too much. She whirled and exclaimed in a trembling voice, "Rebecca is not my mamma! My mother is Jane Horner. Don't ever call her mother to me again."

She turned and stooped to rouse Jonathan.

"Young lady!" her father shouted, upsetting a stool as he rushed toward her. "I'll teach you—"

Rebecca's firm voice interrupted. "Edward. No."

Sarah Jane looked defiantly at her father. He glared at her a moment before he stalked out.

Her defiance threatened to dissolve in tears, and Sarah Jane bit her lips to control herself as she helped Jonathan dress. When her lips no longer trembled and her eyes were dry, she returned to the fireplace.

She held her head high, a challenge to any reprimand her stepmother might have. But Rebecca was giving breakfast preparations her whole attention. She carefully stirred porridge in the iron kettle swung on the crane over the fire. She turned slices of salt pork browning on the griddle. In a matter-of-fact way she handed the fork and spoon to her stepdaughter.

Leaving the breakfast to Sarah Jane's care, Rebecca went outside to help her husband load food to barter— vegetables, eggs, a ham, and honey—into the wagon bed with the three hens and a bag of shelled corn.

When the wagon was packed, Pa silently joined Sarah Jane to gulp breakfast while Rebecca packed lunches for them to eat in Oshkosh. Then he hurried to the wagon. Sarah Jane climbed in, avoiding his glance.

As her father shouted to the oxen and cracked the whip over their heads and they moved down the lane, Sarah Jane looked back at her brother with a twinge of loneliness hurting inside her. For the first time in his life she was going away without him. Jonathan and Rebecca stood hand in hand, waving. Jonathan ran a step or two after the wagon. Then he returned to Rebecca.

Sarah Jane clenched her hands in her lap. "I will never let Jonathan forget our mother," she blurted, as the wagon jolted from the grassy lane into the ruts of the county road.

Expecting another outburst like the one at breakfast, Sarah Jane was dumbfounded by the understanding smile her father flashed at her.

"That's just what Rebecca said," Edward Horner declared. "Never to let Jonathan forget his mother— always keep her memory alive for him. That's why she had me put up that shelf for your mother's picture. 'Never, never,' she said, 'must we rob that little boy of his own mother.' She said, 'Life must go on, but it is up to us to help him keep his own mother.' "

"She said that?" Sarah Jane asked shakily.

"Those were her very words," her father answered. "She had Thomas come to make sure I'd understand about the importance of that shelf. Most usually, we don't have to bother Thomas to interpret, but she thought this concerned you and Jonathan as much as it did her and me, so she asked him to help with the understanding."

Sarah Jane's last thought the night before, her first thought this morning, had been that Rebecca was a calamity in their lives which she must brace herself to fight. What her father was saying made Rebecca seem the very opposite.

While Sarah Jane tried to sort out her thoughts, the oxen plodded slowly through a fragrant tunnel of trees growing so close on either side of the sandy road that they met overhead in a green arch that shut out the fierce burn of the July sun.

Watching the movement of the oxen, she relaxed and settled against her father's shoulder. He patted her hand and interrupted a monotonous little tune he was whistling to smile at her. She gave herself up to the pleasure of his companionship. This was like the dream she had built in her mind during the four lonely years in the orphanage: a dream of loving companionship in a comfortable home made by a capable Sarah Jane for her father and Jonathan.

They came out again into bright hot sunlight. Sarah Jane sat up straighter and pulled her bonnet forward to protect her eyes from the glare.

"Yonder," said her father, gesturing toward a yellow brick building on the right side of the road, "is the school. Not really too far from home, you see, but it will be a tidy walk. That's why you must have sturdy boots."

Sarah Jane studied the compact building wondering uneasily about the children with whom she would be going to school. School in Lincoln had been only a now-and-again thing when she could be spared from her duties to join the other girls in the morning classroom presided over by nearsighted Matron.

Past fields of hay growing golden in the hot sun, past rustling cornfields, the oxen plodded drowsily on. There was a house, and then another wooded stretch. Sarah Jane was more asleep than awake when, with the sun directly overhead, Pa suddenly sat up straighter, adjusted his hat on his head, and fished his wallet from his pocket.

"Fox River up ahead," he said, gesturing with the whip. "Toll bridge coming up takes us over into Algoma

village. Just a little while, and we'll be in Oshkosh—
it's probably three, four miles downstream. When first
I came, we had to cross on a ferry. Run by a man by
the name of Knagg, it was. But last year, or maybe the
year before that, a man named Coon built this bridge.
Easier and quicker now."

Halting on the bank of the wide, swift flowing river,
Pa counted fifty cents into the hand of the waiting
bridgekeeper .

Onto the bridge they went. Sarah Jane glanced down
at the water glinting between the planks. She closed her
eyes quickly because the emptiness of her stomach and
the movement of the water made her dizzy. She relaxed
again when they drove off the bridge.

They were in a little village with a store, a sawmill,
and a few houses. This was Algoma, and it was soon left
behind. After a short ride through grassy meadows along
the river, the wagon rolled onto a busy street with stores
and shops on either side.

"Oshkosh at last," her father announced, smiling
at her.

Sarah Jane sat in the wagon while Edward Horner
left a bag of corn for grinding at the grist mill. She
looked up and down the busy street eagerly. Perhaps
it was to Oshkosh she should come to escape her stepmother's home. Oshkosh was bigger than Stickney, a
village with only one street and stone cottages, thatch
roofed. It was smaller than Lincoln, with its cobbled
streets and old gray buildings crowded close together.
Here in Wisconsin were boardwalks, dusty streets, wooden
buildings. Oshkosh was a strange sight to Sarah Jane's eyes.

None of the passersby paid much attention to her until a group of Indians coming up the street paused. An old man, his white hair accenting the darkness of his skin, leaned against Pa's wagon. A young man slapped the near ox on the flank. His eyes flicked over Sarah Jane, who sat frozen with fear, unable to utter a scream to summon her father to rescue her.

Maudie's words in faraway Lincoln suddenly echoed in her ears: "Don't let those red Indians scalp you and kidnap Jonathan!"

Before she could conquer her pounding heart enough to call for help, Pa was beside the wagon, talking calmly to the two men. He shook hands with a blanketed woman who stood at the back of the wagon, and he knelt a moment to talk to a little boy about Jonny's size.

"Meet my daughter, Sarah Jane," Pa said proudly. "Came to us from England, she and her brother Jonathan. Sairy, this is White Cloud and his father, and Singing Bird, his wife."

Their solemn dark eyes studied her. Sarah Jane was glad they did not expect conversation from her and relieved when they started up the street. Pa goaded the oxen into motion. He drove down the street until they reached the shade of a big elm tree. He stopped the oxen and climbed to the seat beside her to eat the lunch Rebecca had packed for them. He had failed to see how frightened Sarah Jane had been.

"All ready?" Pa asked when their lunch was finished. He held out his hand to help her jump from the wagon. "Let's go find the shop with the most boot for the money."

From shop to shop they went until in the third one,

Pa found what he liked.

Sarah Jane sat down while the shopkeeper measured her feet. He brought a pair of trim brown, ankle-hugging boots. Kneeling, he put them on her feet. She wiggled her toes in the roomy boots, enjoying the leathery smell of newness. Until now, new shoes for her had been someone's outgrown shoes from the orphanage storeroom.

"Well, how about it?" asked her father, beaming proudly. "Think they'll do?"

"They're beautiful, Pa, and so comfortable," she said, wishing that the shopkeeper did not smile so broadly at her.

When they went out into the hot sun of the dusty street, her father said, "Now let's take this basket of sweet corn up to Mr. Burnside to pay him for sending me his Oshkosh True Democrat newspaper. Then we'll go down to Smith's Corner Store to trade for the molasses and rice, codfish and lamp oil Rebecca wants. After that, we'll be starting home."

Sarah Jane followed her father up the stairs to the newspaper office. It was stuffy and dark after the blazing sun on the street. A large man, puffing a cigar, pushed the chair back from his desk. Exclaiming loudly, he came to meet Pa, hands outstretched for the basket of corn Pa was carrying.

"Umm-yumm! Good sweet corn," he said, smacking his lips. "This will keep the Democrat coming your way for four more months, Ed."

The powerful smell of printer's ink and the noise of a small job press two big boys were working across the room made Sarah Jane's head whirl. Near where she stood, a grizzled man slouched in a chair, drunkenly snoring, his head against a typecase.

Sarah Jane stepped back as Pa and Mr. Burnside crossed the room toward her, and she blushed as the big editor held out his hand.

"And is this the little daughter, come at last from England?" he asked loudly as he shook her hand. "We'll put it in the paper that you've come to join us. And how was the trip to Sheboygan, Ed? Did it storm over that way, too?"

Mr. Burnside listened to Pa tell about the rainstorm and the heat and the ships in Sheboygan, the Winnebago locomotive and the plank road meeting at the crowded Wade House inn. At the same time, he deftly selected individual pieces of metal type from the case in front of him.

Sarah Jane bent forward to see what the editor was picking out so quickly. The small blocks had tiny raised letters, but she could not make head or tail of them. Mr. Burnside set the pieces of type line by line in a holder in his left hand. Then he quickly inked the rows of letters and pressed a scrap of paper over them. Carefully he held the still damp result out to her.

"There, you're all ready to appear in the columns of the True Democrat," he said.

The strange looking letters had turned rightside up into clear black lines of type that said, "Sarah Jane, daughter of Ed Horner, south of town, arrived from Stickney, Lincolnshire, England."

"Oh, my brother Jonathan came, too," she said.

With a laugh, Mr. Burnside quickly selected another

line of type, inked it, and printed the words on another scrap of paper. "A son, Jonathan, accompanied his sister."

"Take care, it's messy when the ink's wet," Mr. Burnside warned. "Your ma won't like printer's ink on your nice clean dress."

"My stepmother," Sarah Jane said. But Pa interrupted her quickly to tell Mr. Burnside about his flax crop, and the editor grumbled about Jake and his bottle, gesturing toward the man snoring against the typecase.

Pa peered curiously at the compartments filled with pieces of type in the typecase. "It takes clever hands to do that job of Jake's," he said. "It puts me in mind of weaving." There was a wistful tone to his voice, and Sarah Jane thought suddenly, "Poor Pa! He should be doing clever things with his skillful hands instead of breaking his back with farming."

"Yes, you're right, Ed," said Mr. Burnside. "It takes clever hands and a mind not addled by drink. Don't know what I'm going to do about Jake here." They talked a few moments more, and then Pa led the way down the stairs.

Carefully holding the two scraps of paper still wet with Jonathan's name and hers, Sarah Jane waited outside the door of Smith's Corner Store while Pa bought the things Rebecca needed. Her new boots began to feel heavy and hot on her feet. A boat on the river at the foot of the street blew three loud blasts on its whistle. People hurried down the boardwalk toward the river.

"Jonny would be hurrying to see the boat, too," she thought.

But she stayed where she was, comforted by Pa's

nearness. She had had enough of boats to last her for a long time. She looked at the things in the store window: bolts of calico in red and gray, jars of hard candies, and carpenter's tools, all crowded together.

When Pa had finished his trading, she followed him along the walk to the wagon, enjoying the clatter of her new boots on the planks of the walk. On the slow hot trip home, she drowsed sometimes with her head on Pa's shoulder. Lazily she stretched out her legs to admire the new boots. She wondered what sort of adventures they'd carry her into when she walked up the road to school with Eliza on the first day of summer term.

8 *School*

BRAND NEW BOOTS and the chance to go to real school!
Those new blessings should have made the days before
the opening of summer term happy days for Sarah Jane.
Instead they were troubled days and dream tormented
nights.

Pa was in the fields all day or away trading work
with some other farmer. Sarah Jane alone in the house
with her stepmother, felt lonelier than she had ever felt
in the orphanage in Lincoln. There she had always had
Maudie and the other girls to talk to, or Cook, or even
Matron.

Here she felt penned in a hot cabin and a small
clearing beyond which she was afraid to step, with the
intruder, the foreigner whose language she could not speak.

"Not that I really want to speak to her even if I
could," Sarah Jane said softly one day when she was alone
at the hen yard gate. Feeding the hens, Pa had told her,
was a duty she should take on to help Rebecca. Although
she was afraid of the squawking, pecking, fluttering hens,
she made the duty last as long as possible, for it gave
her a chance to brood without seeming to be lazy.

She wondered as she leaned on the fence watching
the chickens why Pa was so set on the idea Rebecca was

delicate. "My wife's not strong now," he had said to Mrs. Wade. And to Sarah Jane, "You must relieve Rebecca of as many of her burdens as you can until she is stronger." Sarah Jane frowned, thinking that her stepmother seemed strong and healthy enough to her.

Resentment simmered in her, clouding every joy, giving a bitter aftertaste to food, haunting her dreams.

Night after night, Sarah Jane dreamed the old dream of making a good home for Pa and Jonathan. It was the dream that had filled so many nights at the orphanage, only it was more elaborate now. She was presiding over an American house which looked like the Wade inn, in miniature. There was always a sunny parlor and a dining room with peafowl spatterware dishes on the table every day. At a big spinning wheel in the corner Sarah Jane herself expertly worked. Jonathan grew tall and plump and healthy, and Pa lost that lean, worn look. He didn't grumble anymore, and he even grew back his curly hair. Visitors in the dream always said behind their hands when Sarah Jane went to the kitchen to put the teakettle on to boil: "Yes, she takes care of them herself—a wonderful job for a slip of a girl."

And then the dream became a nightmare. An intruder, large and dark like Rebecca, but frowning as Rebecca never frowned, burst into the miniature Wade inn and drove Sarah Jane out. The dream callers said behind their hands: "Yes, she really does need to be a girl. Out with her!"

And Sarah Jane awoke, crying.

In spite of her stiff unfriendliness Sarah Jane noticed that Jonathan was able to carry on quite a conversation with his stepmother. She taught him Welsh words for things, and he taught her English words. He made her say them over and over until he was satified with her pronunciation. And they both laughed together.

Sarah Jane watched them jealously. "She has stolen our mother's place, and now she's trying to steal my little brother from me. I'll never, never let her do it. Oh, I hate her, I hate her!"

Tears filled Sarah Jane's eyes so often that they burned and her head ached. Pa worried about her. Rebecca, concern making her dark eyes larger, felt Sarah Jane's forehead, testing for fever. Because Pa was watching, Sarah Jane dared not jerk away from her stepmother's cool, gentle hands, but she tried after that to control her tears before them.

On the Sunday before school opened for the summer term, Pa woke the family early. "We're going over to the Welsh church," he told Sarah Jane. "We need an early start because our oxen are such slow critters."

Sarah Jane sat glumly alone on the board Pa had laid across the wagon bed as a seat for the children. Before the Horners had been long on the road Jonathan left her to crawl between Pa and Rebecca. To quiet his excited chatter to proper Sunday dignity, Rebecca taught him the Lord's Prayer in Welsh. Even Pa joined in some of the phrases. Sarah Jane felt completely shut out in her loneliness.

The small white-steepled church stood in a clearing among the trees. It was beautiful in the sunshine. Men, women, and children were arriving, some in wagons with oxen like Pa's, others in carriages with horses. Everyone talked quietly in Welsh. Pa did not seem to mind the strange language, and all the people seemed to accept Pa.

The curious eyes turned on Sarah Jane and Jonathan were friendly, but Sarah Jane wished she could hide. Then Eliza Hughes ran across the churchyard toward her, and Sarah Jane turned gratefully to her.

The church service was in Welsh. Sarah Jane could guess at the meaning and say the words in English under her breath, but she resented it when her father joined in the Welsh prayers and songs. It seemed to Sarah Jane that he was denying their whole life by speaking in her stepmother's language.

But as the harmony of the beautiful hymns rose in the little church, it carried Sarah Jane out of her resentment and made her feel fresh. She noticed that her stepmother's voice was the loveliest in the congregation.

After church, invitations to Sunday dinner were pressed upon the Horners. Smiling gratefully, but shaking her head, Rebecca made explanations for the family.

Pa repeated loudly as if saying strange words loudly made them more understandable: "We have the animals to look after, and Sarah Jane has to be all rested and ready for her first day in American school."

When they could not be persuaded to stay, an old, white-haired woman brought a bundle to Rebecca. Unfolding it, she lifted up little garments, one by one, talking rapidly in Welsh all the while.

When the woman had finished speaking and unfolding what looked to Sarah Jane like doll clothes, Rebecca kissed her on the cheek. Still talking rapidly, they worked together, refolding the garments.

"What can this mean?" Sarah Jane wondered, but Eliza ran up to her then, whispering, "I'll see you in the morning." Pa clucked to the oxen and the Horners set off for home and preparations for school. The gift to Rebecca slipped from Sarah Jane's mind.

Father called Sarah Jane early Monday morning. "I want to give you plenty of time with your morning chores on such an important day," he explained.

Rebecca brought Sarah Jane her best red-sprigged calico dress. Even in her best dress and new boots, Sarah Jane felt neither festive nor brave as she picked up the dish of scraps for the chickens.

As she stepped carefully through the dewy grass, she was not sure whether chickens or a school full of strange boys and girls made her heart pound. With their strong wings, sharp beaks, and scaly feet, the hens seemed ferocious and dangerous out of proportion to their size.

Opening the gate, she thrust the dish of scraps into the hen yard. She drew back from the chickens' noisy rush. When they were busily pecking at the food, she reopened the gate and reached for the water dish. But the cock dragging his wings rushed toward her making threatening sounds.

Quickly she shut the gate against him. Puffing out his feathers, stretching his iridescent neck, and scolding her, he ran back and forth behind the gate.

"Oh, you're hateful—you—you Satan, you!" she told him angrily.

A merry laugh made Sarah Jane whirl around, startled. Eliza Hughes had come quietly up the lane. She stood smiling at Sarah Jane.

"You're a good rooster namer, Sarah Jane," Eliza said, laughing again. "Satan is a good name for him. I've always said Uncle Ed's rooster is the meanest in the valley."

"He's mean, all right," Sarah Jane said. "I've got to give those silly chickens water before I can have my breakfast. I don't want to be late my first day at school. I'm scared enough anyway."

Sarah Jane shook the gate at the persistent rooster fussing back and forth before it. He squawked fiercely at her.

"I'll tell you what we'll do," Eliza said. "You fill the water pan while I run to the barn for a handful of grain. I'll scatter it down at the other end of the hen yard. You can slip the water in while they're gobbling up the grain."

It worked as Eliza planned. Laughing at the trick they had played on the rooster, the girls ran to the house. While Sarah Jane ate her breakfast, Eliza sat on the steps, chattering in English to Uncle Ed, in Welsh to Aunt Rebecca.

As the girls started down the lane, Jonathan stood at the door watching. Sarah Jane walked backward, waving to him. He looked so tiny and helpless that Sarah Jane was overwhelmed with the feeling that she was running away from her greatest responsibility.

"We'll have to hurry," Eliza said. "Teacher doesn't like for us to be late, and today she'll want to try you out so she'll know where to put you. I hope we are in the same reader, don't you?"

As Sarah Jane nodded an eager reply, two big boys with book bags, slates, and lunch baskets slung over their shoulders, rushed out of a lane ahead of them. Shouting and laughing, they tossed a ball back and forth across the road. They were tall, noisy fellows, almost full grown. Involuntarily Sarah Jane stepped closer to Eliza who quietly took her hand.

"Those are the Darwin boys," Eliza explained. "They must have finished hoeing corn yesterday. They come to school only when their father doesn't have work for them on the farm. Then they come just because their mother wants them to get an education. It'll take more than sitting in school to educate them! All they do is pester us and sass Teacher."

Boys and girls joined them at each farm they passed. "How many go to school?" Sarah Jane asked, alarmed by the number.

"Thirty-five when we're all there," Eliza said. "But during summer term, the boys are busy in the fields, and sometimes girls have to help, too."

As they approached the yellow brick school, a crowd of children ran into the schoolyard from the north. Sarah Jane could not take her eyes from a tiny girl riding on her big brother's shoulders.

"She's just a baby," Sarah Jane exclaimed to Eliza.

"She'll be four next month," Eliza said. "Those are the Watsons. Their mother has the twins at home, just two years old. Grandpa Watson is sick abed, and Mrs. Watson has to wait on him all the time, so to help his ma Henry brings Lucy May to school. It's real cunning to hear her learn her letters. When she gets too sleepy, Teacher makes up a bed for her on the bench in the back of the room, and Lucy May takes a nap."

"Jonathan is about her size," Sarah Jane said.

"Wouldn't it be nice if he could come, too?"

"Don't let Teacher hear you say that," said Eliza. "She doesn't like to have babies in school. Come on, you must meet Teacher."

Eliza led Sarah Jane toward the young woman standing in the doorway of the school. But Miss Tillie Wallace was already ringing the handbell and there was no time to talk.

Children crowded noisily into the schoolroom. Little ones sat in seats near the small platform where the teacher's desk stood. The big boys clomped to seats at the back, yanking at girls' braids as they passed. Eliza's desk was in the middle of the room, a large double desk. She drew Sarah Jane down beside her.

After reading the Ten Commandments, Miss Wallace set groups of children to work with slates or with copybooks, inkwells, and steel pens. Then she called the Fourth Reader group, Eliza, three other girls, and a boy, to her desk. As they were arranging themselves on the recitation bench, Miss Wallace brought Sarah Jane a slate filled with arithmetic examples.

"Show me how far you can go with these," she told her new pupil, "while I listen to this reading class. After that, we'll see which reader is for you."

Arithmetic! Sarah Jane shuddered. It was always hard for her. Addition she could do with fair assurance, and her subtraction usually made sense. Once in a while her multiplication was right—but her division seldom divided. She wanted so much to do well for the teacher, but with numbers her mind was like a sieve. She rubbed out an incorrect answer for the third time and closed her eyes in despair.

"Sarah Jane! Don't go on to another example until the first one is correct," Miss Wallace said, speaking sharply close to Sarah Jane's shoulder. While Eliza was reading, the teacher had come quietly down the aisle. "Keep your mind on your work."

Impatiently Sarah Jane wrote and erased and wrote again. Nine times seven could never be 81! But it had little chance of being anything else on Sarah Jane's slate when more than half her mind was following the story the girls were reading from the Fourth Reader.

The arithmetic was still unfinished when Miss Wallace called Sarah Jane to the front of the room to read a trial page in the Fourth Reader.

Sarah Jane loved to read. She now passed from book to book without any mistakes until she reached the Eighth Reader, the very last one on Teacher's desk.

"You read very well, Sarah Jane," Miss Wallace said. "Reading is going to be the least of your troubles here. Arithmetic we'll have to work on. You may go to your seat now and share the geography book with Eliza."

When the day was finished, Miss Wallace had assigned Sarah Jane to read with the Eighth Reader class, the biggest boys and girls. She was to do sums with the smallest children, and geography and history, spelling and penmanship with Eliza and the others in her class.

Next day the girl behind her laughed when Sarah Jane went to the blackboard behind Teacher's desk to do sums with the little children. But Sarah Jane would learn to toss her head and laugh back at her. Each day, with Miss Wallace's help, she felt more sure of arithmetic, and she hoped she could soon catch up with her own class.

One schoolday followed another. Each morning, Sarah Jane met Eliza at the end of the lane. The walk to school with her new friend was the happiest part of each day.

As these first weeks in Wisconsin went by, Sarah Jane sometimes felt a little homesick for the old times in England. Matron had been strict, but she'd always praised Sarah Jane for caring for Jonny. Now it was Pa and Rebecca with whom Jonny spent most of his time and to whom he turned for help. Sarah Jane still resented it.

One evening when her father and stepmother had thought she was asleep in her attic room, she overheard them talking as they sat together on the cabin doorstep. The talk was about money and hard times. Her father did most of the talking, much of it to himself. But Sarah Jane realized that she and Jonny must have added greatly to his worries. She wished she were older. Thirteen was not old enough to be independent. If she could look after herself, she'd not be beholden to Pa or his new wife or anyone else. She'd often daydreamed of making a home for Jonny when things had been hard at the orphanage. Now she played again with the idea.

Something else bothered Sarah Jane, too. Suppose that some day there should be a new baby, a halfsister or brother. That would mean an even greater strain on the family's resources. And how would Jonny fare then?

To Sarah Jane, the answer seemed clear. She must go away. She grew more certain of that each day. She could not be loyal to her own mother, she could not be happy herself if she remained in her stepmother's home.

In a way, too, she would be helping her father, for there would be one less person to depend upon him.

One day as Jonathan ran down the lane to meet Sarah Jane when she came home from school she studied his face as if she were seeing him again after a long absence. He was not the pale, thin little boy he had been when they left England. Sunshine and fresh air and good food and peaceful sleep were putting color in his cheeks and a trace of plumpness to hide his bones.

"I'm a helper, Sar' Jane," he chattered, telling her about feeding the chickens and the pigs, about pulling weeds and carrying a drink to Pa in the field. "I'm helping Mummy-Becky to talk like we do—I'm a real helper."

"Do you miss me, Jonny?" Sarah Jane asked jealously.

"Oh, yes, Sar' Jane. We wait and wait for you to come."

Jonathan had been walking backward up the lane ahead of his sister. Now he came to put his hand in hers. "Pa showed me watercress by the brook. Mummy-Becky likes watercress. I get her some every day. Do you like watercress? I'll get you some, too." His words tumbled on. "I picked blackberries and saved the biggest one for Mummy-Becky. You can have some for supper, too. And Mummy-Becky and I learned so many new words. We want to say them for you. I watch and watch for you to come, Sar' Jane."

In the cabin, Rebecca bent over the supper fire, her face flushed. Her smile of welcome was as warm for Sarah Jane as for Jonathan. For a moment Sarah Jane felt shame over her continued unfriendliness toward her stepmother.

"Jonny, the water, please, and Sarah Jane, the table. Then we eat," Rebecca said. They were English words, and easy enough for Sarah Jane to understand, but they had a certain lilt to them.

While Jonathan ran to the spring with the water pail, Sarah Jane set the table. Edward Horner appeared from the hay field at the edge of the clearing. He was tired and hot, but he questioned Sarah Jane about school.

"Sairy learns at school," he said proudly. "And Jonny and Mummy learn here at home. The very best of Americans we're all going to be, eh, Becky?"

Jonny and Rebecca and Edward chattered through the meal, laughing together about the happenings of their day. Sarah Jane sat unsmiling. She was beginning to feel shut out by the closeness that bound her father, Rebecca, and Jonny together. She asked herself if she was being selfish to want to keep Jonny's love, but she decided fiercely that it could not be wrong to keep his love to make sure he remembered his own mother.

The more Sarah Jane thought about Jonny at home while she spent the day at school, the less happy she felt. Certainly Rebecca was kind and loving to the little boy. But that was just the trouble. Then an idea occurred to Sarah Jane and it seemed the answer to her problems.

"There's a little girl at school who's only four," she said suddenly. "The teacher makes a bed on a bench when it's her nap time. She's learning to read and cipher and everything. I could ask Teacher and bring Jonny, too."

Her father drained his cup of tea and set it on the table with a thud. "Yes, that is Hank Watson's girl, and I know why she's in school. There's no sickness in our home to push a little one out too soon. Next year's soon enough for Jonnny."

Sighing, Sarah Jane turned to her evening chores. She fed and watered chickens and pigs. She washed the dishes. Before it was too dark she sat on the step and silently studied her spelling from the book which Miss Wallace had given her.

Her father leaned against the maple tree opposite the door, sharpening the curving blade of the scythe, ready for mowing the next day. Behind her, Rebecca rocked Jonathan, singing a lullaby, a sweet haunting tune with Welsh words.

It was just so that Jane Horner had rocked Sarah Jane, singing in a high tiny voice:

Hush, my child,
Lie still and slumber,
Heavenly angels
Guard thy bed.

Many times Sarah Jane had tried to sing it as she rocked Jonathan when he was small. But even then he had been too big a load for her arms, and her voice was too uncertain to be soothing.

The rhythm and melody of Rebecca's song rose and fell as darkness crept out of the woods which edged the swamp behind the house. Darkness brought a soft cooling breeze to lift the bangs from Sarah Jane's hot forehead. She sighed and let her spelling book drop closed on her lap.

Lulled herself by Rebecca's sweet song, Sarah Jane thought drowsily, "How nice that Jonny has someone who can really sing to him."

Then guilt suddenly overwhelmed her at the disloyalty of her thought. She arose quickly and noisily dropped her book. Snatching it up, her voice was almost rude as she said, "I have to go to bed so I'll not be sleepy in school tomorrow."

Rebecca smiled but put her finger to her lips. Jonathan stirred in her arms and cried out. She sang a phrase and he was quiet again.

Sarah Jane paused for a moment at the little shelf which held her mother's picture before she climbed the ladder to her hot attic room.

"I wish I could earn money to leave more quickly," she whispered as she undressed. "She will make *me* disloyal to Mother, too."

 *9 Disloyalty*

PA AND THOMAS HUGHES were working together harvesting the hay in the big meadow north of the schoolhouse.

It was a hot afternoon. As Sarah Jane and Eliza left the schoolyard, they could see Pa's wagon, heavily loaded with hay, traveling slowly up the road ahead of them.

"Let's run and catch up," Eliza suggested. "It's fun riding on top of the hay."

Pa looked flushed and tired, but he smiled a welcome and stopped the oxen to swing Eliza and Sarah Jane to the top of the load of hay.

The girls could have walked as fast as the oxen went, but it was fun to see the familiar road from the top of the loaded wagon.

Sarah Jane settled back, watching treetops and fluffy clouds in the summer sky. Eliza, softly singing a Welsh song, braided strands of hay into a long rope. Both girls were quiet and drowsy when the wagon came to a stop before the Horner barn. Edward Horner held up his arms to help them slide from the hay to the ground.

"Run help your mamma with the supper things," he said to Sarah Jane. "I want to eat quickly and be off to the field to get another load of hay before I go to bed."

Eliza bounded off across the marsh shortcut to the Welsh settlement. Sarah Jane stood a moment brushing wisps of hay from her dress and hair. She whispered stubbornly to herself, "I'll help, but she's *not* my mamma!"

Her father followed her to the house, still talking, "Becky will be doing the milking for me tonight, too, so you give her extra help around the house."

Jonathan hopped from the cabin as Sarah Jane entered. "Hello, Sar' Jane," he called importantly over his shoulder. "I'm a pig feeder tonight. Mummy-Becky is very busy so I am a pig feeder just like a man." Sarah Jane smiled as she watched Jonathan stagger down the path holding the bucket before him.

She joined Rebecca in the last minute rush of supper preparation. Beans boiling in the iron pot on the crane over the fire had to be tested and seasoned. Sarah Jane set the table.

The meat pie in the stone oven in the dooryard was ready. When Sarah Jane opened the oven door she saw that there were also blackberry turnovers, golden crusted, the rich dark juice of berries bubbling up through the pricks dotting the crust in the shape of an H. Rebecca set them to cool while Sarah Jane, stepping carefully, carried the heavy meat pie to the table.

No chatter prolonged supper. Pa ate and returned to haying. Rebecca went to the barn to milk the cow. Sarah Jane hurriedly washed dishes and tidied the room. Then she sat with the slateful of arithmetic examples on the step where she could keep a watchful eye on Jonathan sailing chip boats in the brook.

Rebecca finished milking and tucked Jonathan into

the trundle bed. With her knitting, she came to sit on the doorstep. Too late, Sarah Jane wiped away tears. Not even the first example had the correct answer when she tried to prove it.

"Trouble with numbers?" Rebecca asked.

"Yes," Sarah Jane exclaimed. "Numbers never go right for me."

"Maybe I—help—?" Rebecca said hesitantly.

Sarah Jane was already unhappy, and her stepmother's faltering English only annoyed her. Rebecca used more English words each day and spoke more understandably, thanks to Jonathan's persistence, but she still groped for words and put sentences together in strange order.

Rebecca continued, "Numbers for me—easier—than words. Come, the light, and maybe I help."

Sarah Jane could not refuse the offer she knew was well meant. She brought her slate to the table where Rebecca was shading the lamp so that Jonathan was not disturbed.

"Maybe," Rebecca went on, "I help you with numbers. You help me with words?"

Suddenly Sarah Jane was ashamed of her impatience with her stepmother's awkward speech. She pushed the slate to Rebecca, who bent over it for a moment. She quickly found the mistakes.

Moving from example to example, Sarah Jane worked, following Rebecca's finger as she pointed out the mistakes. The time passed quickly.

When the arithmetic was finished and checked, they paused, listening for the sound of hoofs or the creak of wheels in the hot darkness. Insects shrilled in the night. The trees stirred in the slight breeze, rustling with that harsh sound leaves make when days have too long been hot and dry. There was a slight movement in the air, but little relief from the heat.

Sarah Jane pushed aside the slate and opened her spelling book. "Uncle Thomas tells me I should help you learn English," she said. "You helped me with my arithmetic. Maybe I can help you with my spelling words."

Sarah Jane stopped suddenly, wondering if Rebecca understood. But she had noticed before that her stepmother seemed to understand more than she could put into words.

Rebecca, smiling slightly, nodded and moved her stool closer so that they could both read from the page. Underlining with her finger, Sarah Jane slowly read each word in the spelling assignment and each definition. Falteringly, Rebecca read each word after her.

They went through the whole list of words. With *deference* and *difference* and *ingenuous* and *ingenious* Rebecca struggled. She pressed the palm of her left hand against her forehead in a little gesture of despair, the gesture Sarah Jane had seen before when Pa scolded and grumbled.

"But you don't need to be discouraged," Sarah Jane reassured her. "You say the words better than a lot of the boys and girls at school. And it's not even your language."

"Oh, yes—my language it is now, too," Rebecca said heatedly.

Sarah Jane recognized the spirit in that answer. "Well," she said, "Jonny has helped you a lot already.

And I'll help you all I can and it *will* be your language."

"Dear Sarah Jane!" Rebecca said, and a wave of shame and embarrassment made Sarah Jane's face hotter. Her stepmother's gratitude for the pronouncing of some easy words made her realize how unfriendly she had been and how ungrateful for all the things Rebecca silently did for them all. She drew the book closer to her and bent over it to hide her feelings.

"I have to get my spelling for tomorrow. We'll read the words once more, and then I'll spell them for you. You tell me if I am right, please."

"Yes, good," Rebecca agreed.

They chanted the words and their definitions jerkily, syllable by syllable. Then Rebecca took the book while Sarah Jane spelled the words for her. They were drilling over and over on *lineament, a feature; liniment, an ointment* and *principal, chief; principle, rule of action,* the bothersome words for Sarah Jane, when unannounced by hoofbeats or creaking wheels, Edward Horner stepped through the door.

He sat down wearily on the stool across the table from them, mopping his face with his sleeve. Sarah Jane ran through the dark to the springhouse to bring a pitcher of cold buttermilk for him.

When she returned he was explaining, "It was too late to come home with the load. We tethered the oxen on the edge of the meadow. It will give them extra rest— lean beasts that they are—so they'll be fresher for tomorrow. I rode home behind Tom. Did you have a good evening? You sounded like an old chanting school as I came in."

"She was helping me with my examples," Sarah Jane said. "And I helped her learn my spelling words."

"But now, to bed," said Rebecca. "Tomorrow is school so soon."

As Sarah Jane crossed the room to the attic ladder, her candle illuminated the little tintype of her mother. She looked at it, and a different guilt swept over her. She and Rebecca had been so companionable before the very picture of her own mother! She could not bear the thought of being so disloyal. In bed, she tossed for what seemed like hours before sleeping.

She had not been asleep long when she awoke, coughing. Smoke filled the darkness. Fear for Pa and Jonathan and Rebecca stabbed her mind, and she ran to peer down the opening into the room below. But all was quiet and dark there. She realized then that the smoke came from somewhere beyond the house.

Running to the north window, she peered out and cried in alarm. The whole northwestern sky was orange and flame filled! Frightened, she swung down the ladder, slipping and sliding, hanging by her hands as she missed a step in the dark. Bumping blindly against the edge of the trundle bed, she reached her father. She shook his shoulder.

"Pa, Pa!" she whispered, close to his ear. "Fire! There's a terrible fire!"

Edward Horner leaped to his feet before he was completely awake. At that moment there was the sound of hoofs coming up the lane. Cattle bellowed. Stumbling over the trundle bed, he clumsily pulled on his trousers and ran to the doorway.

"Ted and Ned home by themselves!" he exclaimed, stepping into the yard. "It looks as if the whole meadow and the hay field out beyond the north marsh must be afire."

"Oh!" Sarah Jane tried to say more, but her teeth chattered. "I— I thought at first it was our barn."

She stepped down into the yard with her father. He caught at Ted's dragging rope and succeeded in tethering him to the maple tree at the corner of the barn. Then it was easier to calm Ned.

Suddenly he said, "But there's a whole row of farms in range of that fire, and the schoolhouse, too!"

Rebecca joined them, clutching a shawl around her shoulders. "How far does it come? The houses around the school— are they all right?"

"I can't tell from here," Pa answered. The helplessness and alarm in his voice frightened Sarah Jane.

As they stood watching, the fiery glow gradually died. Soon hoofbeats sounded, pounding down the county road from the north. Thomas Hughes appeared out of the darkness. His horse tossed its head nervously. Dismounting, he looked quickly toward the tethered oxen.

"Oh! It's home they came, thank God!" he exclaimed. "When I could not find your oxen to plow a firebreak, I was afraid we'd find them burned to death in the morning. Your hay is gone, Ed, and the wagon under it. Nothing left of it but the hardware."

"My wagon gone! And not a penny saved to buy another!"

Sarah Jane heard the note of despair. Rebecca put her hand comfortingly on her husband's shoulder. She turned to her brother. "The farmers and their families—the school? Are they— safe?"

"So far as I know. Nothing's lost but the hay and Ed's wagon," Thomas Hughes said. "Evans and I plowed a firebreak. We stopped the fire before I left. Nothing more now but to wait for daybreak and go on from there."

They stood together quietly, the smoke gradually blowing away. Saluting them gravely, Thomas Hughes mounted his horse and disappeared down the dark lane.

The Horners returned to bed. The little boy had slept through the excitement.

It was Jonathan who roused Sarah Jane in the morning. Sar' Jane!" he scolded. "Don't be so slow. Pa had a fire last night. He has to hurry. Come to b'fast."

Her father was finishing his oatmeal when Sarah Jane followed Jonathan down the ladder.

"Forgive me, daughter," he said. "I must get an early start to see if there's anything I can salvage from that wagon. Loss of a whole load of hay bodes no good for the hungry days of winter either. But a wagon gone, that can't be suffered. I'll hike to Oshkosh to arrange for a new wagon. A farmer must have a wagon even if he can't well see how it's to be paid for."

Something flashed in Sarah Jane's mind brighter than last night's fire. "Maybe," she said, suddenly inspired, "I could go to Oshkosh with you and get work somewhere to help you buy another wagon."

"That wagon's for me to worry about," her father said quickly. "You have more important things to worry your head about."

"Please, Pa, let me go!" Her voice shook. "I'm old

enough."

He shook his head, and turning, busied himself with preparations for the trip to Oshkosh.

Addressing her stepmother, Sarah Jane pleaded, "Make him let me go!"

"No, dear," Rebecca said, leading Sarah Jane to her place at the table. "School is your duty now."

With her father and her stepmother in agreement it was useless to continue the argument. Sarah Jane gulped her breakfast and ran down the lane to meet Eliza, who was waiting impatiently.

10 *Red Indians*

A PALL OF SMOKE still hung over the schoolhouse from the blackened meadows beyond the road. No one started a ball game. The boys and girls stood before the schoolhouse door discussing the fire.

"My pa says those good-for-nothing Indians prob'ly started it," declared Gus Schultz.

"How's anyone to tell?" argued Eliza. "My pa says it was so far to the northwest that we can't be sure what started it."

"Aw, any meanness comes from the Indians," said Gus loudly. "Meannesss is their second name. My pa says we ought to drive 'em off our land and shoot those that won't go."

"Oh, no!" Sarah Jane protested, shocked. "You can't shoot people."

"Who says Indians are people?" scoffed Myrtie Schmidt.

"Of course they're people," Sarah Jane and Eliza chorused at the same time.

"Well, mighty dirty, mean ones," Myrtie retorted. "Of course Sarah Jane hasn't been here long enough to understand about things. But you certainly ought to know better, Eliza Hughes. Look how they stole that little Partridge boy. If that isn't mean, I don't know what it is."

A stolen boy? Sarah Jane turned questioningly to Eliza.

"It wasn't the Partridge boy the Indians had. It was their own child," Eliza said. "My pa says the Partridge boy probably drowned in quicksand somewhere and they'll never ever see him again."

"The posse said it was so the Partridge boy," Gus said stubbornly.

"Mrs. Partridge didn't think it was her little boy when the posse brought him to her," Eliza said, her eyes flashing as she argued with the school bully. "My ma says any mother will know her own child, even if he is dirty."

Miss Wallace rang the bell, and the argument was silenced. Sarah Jane, however, sat unheeding through the opening exercises. If the red Indians were child snatchers, how could she ever be certain that Jonathan was safe? Maybe Myrtie's story, not Eliza's, was true. Tales she'd heard in England came back to her, too.

Worrying about Jonathan, Sarah Jane could not keep her mind on arithmetic that morning. As the hot day stretched on, she had a hard time holding her eyes open. She had had so little sleep last night. . . . What was Jonathan doing now? . . . Her imagination took over—Was he stolen and carried away by thieving Indians?

At noontime everyone ate lunch quickly and entered into a lively game of keep-away with the big ball—everyone except Emma Evans and Sarah Jane.

Emma never played rough games. She preferred

to sit in the shade with her knitting. Sarah Jane felt too tired to join the game. She climbed the top rail of the fence beside Emma. In her lunch basket beneath the bread and cold beef were two blackberry turnovers Rebecca had baked in the out-oven with the meat pie yesterday.

"There are two turnovers in my lunch," Sarah Jane said. "Would you like one?"

Emma tucked her knitting in her pocket and took the little pastry. "Your stepma is such a good cook," she said between bites. "My maw says it's a pity she's dumb when she can cook so well and keep such a good house."

Sarah Jane stared at Emma. "She is not dumb!" she said.

"Well, stupid then," Emma insisted. "All she can do is jabber in Welsh. The rest of us Welshmen learned English."

"She is not either stupid," Sarah Jane said indignantly. "You should see her doing my examples for me, quick as ever Teacher does them. And she's learning English more and more every day. My brother teaches her lots of words, and she is learning my spelling words every day, too."

Emma licked the blackberry juice from her fingers. She hadn't had the last word yet. "Well, my paw says he wonders why in the world Mr. Edward Horner wanted to marry someone odd like that."

"My own mother was so lovely that my father would never have married again if he hadn't found someone just as lovely," Sarah Jane said quickly. "And she is a kind person. She is so good to my brother."

Sarah Jane stopped, surprised to find herself defending her stepmother. She'd been so busy resenting her!

Much as she disliked having anyone in her own mother's place, Sarah Jane could never agree to call her stepmother stupid. Odd? Perhaps yes, perhaps no. Oddness was an odd thing itself, she decided. Just when was odd really odd and when was it—well, different? And how dull the world would be without the different!

When Sarah Jane thought of how her stepmother had brought merriment to Jonathan's solemn face, sparkle to his eyes, color to his cheeks, and plumpness to his body, Sarah Jane knew that much as she hated to have Rebecca in her mother's place, impossible as it seemed for Sarah Jane to love her stepmother, she could never agree that this woman was stupid.

Emma's attention was on her knitting, and the conversation dropped. Suddenly Sarah Jane's fears about Jonathan's safety came flooding back. What if the red Indians should steal Jonathan as Gus said they had taken the little Partridge boy?

Emma had finished counting her stitches, so Sarah Jane asked, "What really did happen to that little boy? Where was he stolen? Did the Indians really take him?"

"Caspar Partridge?" Emma asked, knitting rapidly. "Partridges live in Vinland, across the Fox River, over north of Oshkosh. He went to sugar camp with his father and he disappeared. They never found him again."

"Oh, how awful!" exclaimed Sarah Jane.

"And then," Emma went on, "about a year ago some folks saw a little boy in an Indian camp off down toward

Illinois. They thought he looked like Caspar Partridge so they snatched him and brought him back to the Partridges. But when Mrs. Partridge saw him, she said right off that it wasn't her child. And my maw, same as Eliza's maw, says that a mother will know her own child even if he is dirty as anything."

Emma finished her row. Tucking the knitting in her pocket, she jumped carefully to the ground. Sarah Jane jumped down beside her.

"Was it really her child?" Sarah Jane prompted Emma.

"Well, a lot of people, even old Mrs. Partridge, tried to talk young Mrs. Partridge into saying it was her boy, until finally she said, 'Well, maybe.'"

"Oh, it wouldn't be *maybe*!" Sarah Jane protested. "I'd know Jonny for sure, and he's my brother."

Emma nodded. "The Indians came back then, too, and they said he is really the child of Nahkom. The chief—that's Oshkosh, him that the town is named for—he remembers that the little boy is sure enough Nahkom's baby because he was in camp the night that baby was born."

The girls went to take their place in the line for a drink at the pump. Sarah Jane gulped hers quickly and waited impatiently while Emma drank slowly.

"The judge listened to what everyone said," Emma went on as she hung the dipper on its nail. "He decided that the little boy really is Indian Nahkom's, like all the Indians said. But then the posse stole the little boy from the Indians again. And they never did find him after that. So Mrs. Partridge doesn't have her child, and neither does Nahkom."

The bell called the girls to afternoon classes. Sarah Jane's arithmetic examples were meaningless squiggles on her slate. And she couldn't keep her mind on reading, which she loved.

When school was at last over, Sarah Jane started home along the dusty road. In her worry about Jonathan she could not attend to what Eliza was saying. She left her at the gate with only the briefest good-bye.

Jonathan did not meet her in the lane. The house was quiet, and the yard empty. Sarah Jane remembered with apprehension that her father had gone to Oshkosh today to get a new wagon.

Suddenly she clapped her hand over her mouth. Sitting before the cabin door was an old man—an Indian!

He was talking to another, younger, Indian who leaned against the door. Had they already stolen Jonathan and maybe murdered Rebecca?

In her panic Sarah Jane did not recognize the White Cloud family to whom Pa had introduced her in Oshkosh the day she got her new boots.

Before Sarah Jane could decide whether she should run down the lane for help, her stepmother came calmly out of the barn. Sarah Jane rushed toward her, pale with fright.

"What have they—what did they do with Jonny?" she cried. Then she stopped, all at once feeling foolish. Her stepmother was smiling and cradling a blanket-wrapped bundle in her arms. From it came crying sounds.

"Wha-what—why—where?" Sarah Jane stammered

as the young Indian man came quickly across the yard to look at what Rebecca held so tenderly. The older man followed slowly.

"Boy?" White Cloud asked, and received a nod in answer.

"I take him to the house. He needs a—a garment, yes?" Rebecca said, bending down so that Sarah Jane might see the newborn baby.

But Sarah Jane had scant time for him. An Indian baby! A quick glance showed that his face was only a little redder than Jonathan's had been, and a mass of black hair covered his head.

"But where is Jonny?" demanded Sarah Jane as she followed her stepmother to the house.

"He and the White Cloud boy—they ride on the pony," Rebecca told Sarah Jane as she laid the Indian baby on the bed. From the chest she lifted out the small clothes Sarah Jane had seen being given to Rebecca in the Welsh churchyard.

"But—but why?" Sarah Jane's voice rose in renewed anxiety. Jonathan on a pony? "But where is Jonathan? Is he all right?"

"But of course," Rebecca said, straightening with the baby in her arms. She rocked him gently until his crying hushed.

Sarah Jane went to the door, whispering under her breath, "Jonathan, Jonathan!" She wanted to see him now, this minute, with her own eyes. But no one was in sight.

She only half listened as her stepmother tried in her halting broken English to explain that the Indians had been caught by the grass fire while they camped to wait for the birth of Singing Bird's baby. Scarcely attending, Sarah Jane understood that her father had invited the Indian family to stay in his barn when he met them on the Oshkosh road. The baby boy was born, and now Rebecca was clothing him in the garments Sarah Jane had thought were doll clothes when she'd first seen them.

There was a clatter of animals and a chatter of voices in the yard. Running to the door, Sarah Jane saw Jonathan and a little Indian boy mounted on a pony riding into the yard. Behind them came Pa, home from Oshkosh, driving the new wagon, huge, and painted green.

Edward Horner jumped stiffly from the high seat of the wagon. He shook hands with the two Indians, as he had in Oshkosh. Sarah Jane remained in the doorway, watching the three men as they examined the wagon, talking together in the twilight.

Jonathan and his little Indian friend climbed to the seat of the wagon and swung their feet, chattering and laughing together. Rebecca disappeared into the barn with the baby. When she returned, she stood beside her husband, admiring the new wagon.

As Sarah Jane watched Jonathan on the wagon seat with the Indian boy, she began to laugh at how wild and foolish her fears had been. Lack of rest the night before, the heated talk against Indians at school, and the vivid story about the loss of little Caspar Partridge had upset her beyond reason and good sense.

Her laughter at herself changed to hysterical tears. She fled to the house and sat quickly on a stool before the table, burying her face in her crossed arms.

Even when Pa and Rebecca and Jonny came into the house, talking excitedly about the new wagon, Sarah Jane could not stop her tears. Rebecca bent over Sarah Jane, murmuring a strange soft word Sarah Jane could not understand.

"What is the matter, daughter?" Edward Horner asked, perplexed. He shook her shoulder gently, and when she still could not control her sobs, he put his hands under her elbows and pulled her up to face him. "Tell me," he urged. "Are you sick?"

"Oh, no, Pa. Not that. I was so frightened! Jonathan wasn't here and I thought—I thought he was like that Partridge boy. They told me about him at school."

"Oh, no, no!" exclaimed her stepmother, turning from the fireplace where she had been serving up the supper.

Edward Horner sat in the rocker and drew Sarah Jane to his lap. He rocked slowly, stroking her hair away from her hot face. It was as if she were a child, not a strong girl of thirteen.

"Idle talk can cause more fears and raise more trouble than anything I know of, Sairy," her father said slowly. "That was a sad thing about Alvin Partridge's little boy. Judge Buttrick gave it an honest trial, and he's convinced that the Indians never did have little Caspar. Indians are good and bad, same as the rest of us. And White Cloud and Singing Bird are good people, Sairy. They have been good friends to us. Jonathan wasn't in any danger from them."

He rocked gently until her sobbing ceased. "Be good neighbors and you get good neighbors, be the skin red, be the skin white. Remember that, daughter."

When her stepmother called them to supper, Sarah Jane slipped from her father's lap, wiping her hand quickly across her red eyes.

"Think you can stop worrying about Jonathan's being another Caspar Partridge?" Pa asked quietly.

Sarah Jane nodded. But she was exhausted by the long hours and scrambled happenings of that day and she could hardly eat for yawning. When she went to her nightly task of clearing the table, her stepmother shook her head. She put her arm around Sarah Jane and led her to the attic ladder, saying "Too long this day. Sleep now, my child, and peace go with thee."

11 *Sickness*

WHILE SINGING BIRD rested the next day after the birth of her baby, White Cloud and Edward Horner worked together. They cut trees in the woods beyond the cornfield, hauling the logs, sawing them, and stacking the wood along the south side of the cabin. It was the Horners' winter fuel supply.

The old Indian man dozed in the sunshine before the cabin doorstep. He was there when Sarah Jane left for school in the morning, still there when she returned in late afternoon. The two little boys played happily along the brook or rode together on the pony. Rebecca and Singing Bird seemed to communicate without being able to speak many words in each other's language. Sarah Jane felt lonely on the edge of all the good fellowship.

"Be good neighbors, you get good neighbors," Pa had said to her. But her shyness and jealousy each time Jonathan ran to their stepmother with some new discovery kept Sarah Jane a prisoner of her own unfriendliness.

On the third day after the fire, the White Cloud family prepared to leave. Edward Horner shook hands with the young man, thanking him for his help. Rebecca and Singing Bird embraced. The Horners stood together at the head of the lane, waving as the Indians rode away toward the north.

"I wish he didn't have to go," said Jonathan, waving at the little boy mounted on the horse behind his mother. "He's my friend."

As she turned to gather her school things, Sarah Jane thought, "Jonny is a friend to everyone. I should learn to be like him."

Before she could pack her school lunch, Pa, seated at the table drinking a cup of tea before he started the day's work, stopped her.

"Until the flaxseed is safe, I need you here, Sairy," he said apologetically. "I know it isn't right to keep a girl from her lessons, but that flax is my cash crop."

"Oh, but Pa, that's why I'm here, to help," she said. "I can practice spelling and multiplication tables while I work. Lots of pupils are helping at home now anyway."

As she turned to go upstairs to change into her old work dress she kissed her father on the shiny, sunburned spot on the top of his head. Jonathan laughed, and Pa's answering chuckle relaxed the frown that crossed his face too often.

"Truly I'm grateful, daughter," Pa said when Sarah Jane joined him at the edge of the flax field. "Rebecca's been working too hard lately. I'd lose the flax, every seed of it, before I'd risk her coming into the field."

Sarah Jane wondered at this statement, but her father was busy explaining that flax must be pulled and carried to the barn floor for threshing. He showed her how to grasp the stalks below the heads as she braced her heels on the dry ground. She strained to uproot the plants, and her arms ached from the effort. When the flax roots finally came free from the soil, she sat down suddenly.

At first she had only a few stalks of flax for her efforts, and her hands were soon cut by the tough stems. But she gained the knack of uprooting each clump of stalks, even though her hands became red and blistered.

The next day Rebecca came to the barn to tie the flax into bundles. Sarah Jane helped Pa draw a large wooden comb through the dried blossoms. Rippling the flax, he called the process. They were separating the seeds from the pods onto a clean sheet spread on the barn floor.

Rebecca breathed heavily. But she did not stop until her husband sent her to the house.

"Such a little bit of seed for so much work," Sarah Jane complained at the end of the day.

"If I could save some for planting next season," Pa said, pausing to mop his brow, "a second season we might do better. But I have promised all of this crop in payment on the wagon. You run into the house now. Clean up and help Becky with supper."

Rebecca was bending over the fireplace. Sarah Jane said to Rebecca's back, "It's always going to be better *next* season. Why can't it be better *now*? I thought that's why we came to America—to find a better living."

Rebecca did not answer. Tired and cross, Sarah Jane scrambled up the ladder to change into a flax free dress. "No, it won't be better," she concluded. "It's never going to be better in this house where no one can talk to anyone else." She jerked her clean dress so roughly that the arm-hole seam split.

Supper was a silent meal. Everyone seemed tired

and discouraged, and Rebecca ate almost nothing.

As Sarah Jane washed the dishes a glance at Rebecca gave her reason to worry. Feverish spots burned in her stepmother's cheeks and dark circles underlined her eyes. As soon as Jonathan was settled in the trundle bed, Rebecca herself went to bed.

"Everything will be all right in the morning," Sarah Jane tried to tell herself. Nevertheless she tossed and worried during the night. Why had she been so disagreeable? She dreamed of the night her own mother died. She awoke, still feeling anxious, as sunrise streaked the sky.

She was dressed and was making her bed when her father appeared at the top of the ladder.

"I'm glad you're up," he whispered. "Rebecca is sick this morning. I have to go to Oshkosh to make the payment on the wagon, but she should not be up and about today. Would you mind missing school to take care of things here at home?"

Remembering her stepmother's flushed face of the night before, fear flared anew in Sarah Jane's mind. "Of course I'll stay. What—what is the matter? How sick is she?"

"It's chills and fever," he explained. "I've given her the last of the powders the doctor left when I was sick. I must get more today. But I think she should stay in bed."

Sarah Jane hurried down the ladder and stirred the banked fire on the hearth so vigorously that she scattered ashes and blew a puff of smoke into the room.

"I'll have breakfast when you're back from milking," she whispered to her father since Rebecca appeared to be sleeping and Jonny had not wakened. But as Edward Horner stepped from the cabin door with the clatter of milk pail there was a movement in the bed corner. Rebecca was standing by the bed, but she sat down suddenly, holding her head dizzily.

"You must stay in bed!" Sarah Jane said, hurrying across the room. Rebecca hesitated a moment, holding her head. Then she lay down and allowed Sarah Jane to pull the sheet over her.

"Don't try to get up again," Sarah Jane said firmly. "I'm going to be here today. You must stay in bed. Do you understand me?"

Rebecca nodded and smiled faintly. She lightly touched Sarah Jane's hand and spoke with effort, "Fry the cornmeal from yesterday."

Grateful for the suggestion, Sarah Jane set the griddle on the coals. She sliced strips of salt pork to fry first, then she turned out the cold meal on the slicing board. But neither meal nor knife behaved as well as they did in Rebecca's expert hands.

Jonathan awoke then. He was surprised when he saw Rebecca in bed. As he noisily collected his clothes from the stool beside the fireplace, Sarah Jane hushed him.

"We must let her rest today," Sarah Jane told him. "I'm going to do the work and you can be my helper."

"I'm a good helper, Mummy-Becky says," he said in a loud whisper. In his eagerness, he knotted shoelaces, buttoned his shirt askew, and tangled his suspenders. By the time Sarah Jane had put him together properly, Pa came in with the pail of warm, foaming milk.

As Sarah Jane hurried to set out the milk pans with

the clean straining cloth for her father, her nose warned her that the breakfast was overcooking. It was a poor meal, for she had burned some of the slices of meal. She felt unhappy at wasting good food.

Then Pa to his usual grace added in a rush of words, "And we thank Thee for this daughter who serves us so well in our hour of need." From the bed, Rebecca echoed his amen. Sarah Jane sat straighter, the pleasure of being appreciated warming her.

As soon as breakfast was over, Edward Horner set off for Oshkosh with the precious flaxseed. "I'll stop by and tell Miss Wallace not to expect you today," he promised.

Sarah Jane called Jonathan to carry the pan of scraps to the chickens. "You'll have to do it yourself, Jonny," she told him. "I'm as busy as I ever can be in the house."

"I can do it. I'm a big helper boy," Jonathan assured her, and he added, "Mummy-Becky says so."

Sarah Jane washed the dishes, thinking a bit sadly of how naturally and happily Jonathan said "Mummy-Becky." Those words could never come easily from her mouth. As Sarah Jane hung the dishpan behind the door, Jonathan came screaming down the path.

"They're out! They're out! They got away from me, and the old gate tipped over!"

Sarah Jane rushed out, trying to hush Jonathan. Behind him, the cock and hens were hopping over the toppled gate to feed in yard and garden.

"They are naughty chickens," Jonathan sobbed.

"Oh, Jonny!" Sarah Jane cried, but he looked so crestfallen that she could not scold him.

At that moment, Rebecca's voice came from the doorway. "No matter. Jonathan, watch to chase them from the garden patch. At night they will go home to roost."

She leaned weakly against the door casing. Sarah Jane ran to help her back to bed. "You must not get up with every noise we make. Pa will never forgive me if you are worse tonight."

Rebecca lay quietly for a moment, breathing heavily, with her eyes closed. She kept a grasp on Sarah Jane's hand. "It's not your noise. I remember before the noise, the bread! I set the sponge yesterday. Time to stir in the flour and lard and honey and set on top the out-oven to rise in the sun. And today is churning. Abed I must not stay!"

"I'll do it, I can do it all for you!" Sarah Jane cried. "Just tell me what you want me to do."

After smoothing the sheet and fluffing up Rebecca's pillow, Sarah Jane ran to the chimney shelf for the pan of bread sponge. Following directions, she melted lard and stirred it and honey into the yeasty, bubbly sponge. A bit at a time she added flour, vigorously stirring after each addition.

The sponge grew more difficult to handle. Sarah Jane's arm ached from wielding the big wooden spoon through the stiffening batter. When she turned the mass of dough out on the floured table she learned that kneading was even harder than stirring. How did her step-mother ever keep the dough so firm and round as she kneaded?

When she finally had a lopsided ball of dough

greased and sitting at the bottom of the rising pan Sarah Jane eyed it with doubt, wondering if it would make bread fit to eat.

She placed the pan on the top of the out-oven where the heat of the sun would make the dough rise. When she had tidied the kitchen table, which was never so messy after Rebecca mixed bread, Sarah Jane set the stone churn in the shade beside the doorstep. She poured the cream into it. Churning which some days seemed monotonous was a welcome rest after the struggle with breakfast and bread mixing.

Before the butter came Sarah Jane noticed from her place in the shade at the north end of the cabin that the bread, sorry looking lump that it was, had behaved like proper bread set into action by Rebecca's capable hands. It was forcing the covering towel higher and higher as it rose.

"Jonny," Sarah Jane called. "Come churn for me while I poke down the bread. Just one more rising and then I'll make it into loaves. We'll have hot bread for supper when Pa comes home."

Sarah Jane laughed as the high, light bread dough collapsed with an audible sigh when she thrust her fist into it. The mass of dough was more responsive to her hands than it had been earlier. She left it to rise a second time.

"Butter's coming! Butter's here," Jonathan called excitedly.

"Sure enough," she said, pleased to feel the solid pressure of butter against the dasher. She lifted the heavy churn to the kitchen table, ready to work the butter in the

111

big wooden bowl.

Buttermaking was another of the tasks which looked easy as a sneeze when Rebecca did it, but was awkward when Sarah Jane tried. Lumps of butter floating in the buttermilk slipped from the paddle each time she tried to bring them into the ball of butter.

When she was sure she had captured all the butter, she lifted the churn to pour the buttermilk into the big yellow earthenware pitcher. The butter came out with a rush as she poured the milk—it bounced off the edge of the pitcher and would have slithered to the floor if Jonathan had not stopped it with his grimy hands.

Her brother giggled as Sarah Jane scooped up the slippery butter and slapped it into the big wooden butter bowl.

"It isn't funny, Jonny," Sarah Jane declared, nearer tears than she wanted him to know.

As she hurried to the springhouse with the pitcher of buttermilk she noticed many sizable lumps of butter still floated in the liquid. Her father would scold as he did when she pared too thick a peeling from a potato. He'd say, "A careless woman throws away with a teaspoon more than a man can bring in with a shovel."

After she had fastened the springhouse door and was returning to the house she saw that several of the hens had gone to the henhouse.

"The hens are going to their nests to lay their eggs," she told Jonathan as she picked up the butter paddle. "If we watch carefully, maybe they'll all go back and we can shut the gate before Pa gets home."

The sun was high overhead, and Jonathan was begging for something to eat before Sarah Jane had the patty of butter salted and ready to press into the mold. She interrupted her work to give Jonny bread and fresh butter.

She liked Rebecca's butter mold with R for Rebecca on the top. Smoothing butter into the mold seemed the easiest thing in the world when Rebecca did it. But Sarah Jane discovered again that things were rarely as simple as they appeared. She could not get the mold completely filled with butter, so her blocks came out imperfect. When she had finished, she had only three ragged patties of butter. Rebecca usually set away four patties after each churning.

"The bread peeks at me over the top of the pan," Jonathan called as Sarah Jane hurried to put the butter in the springhouse.

Sarah Jane sighed as she stepped into the cool twilight of the springhouse and pulled the door shut after her. With the butter finished, she wished she could sit down to rest for a few minutes. But the bread must be made into loaves to be ready for supper.

She stopped to drink from the cool spring, dipping the water up with the long-handled graniteware dipper hung on a peg.

Cackling of hens in the yard and Jonathan's frantic call cut short her pleasure. She hurried out.

Jonathan rushed toward her screaming, "The naughty old chickens are eating the new bread! I can't make them let go."

Chickens flew squawking and cackling past Sarah Jane and Jonathan toward the out-oven.

"Look!" said Jonathan. "They ate with their mouths,

peck-peck! And they made the tall, fat bread go down, poof! Now they've jumped in with all their feet."

Jonathan was right! Two hens and the cock were standing in the dough, pecking greedily. They squawked and fluttered their wings, trying to fight each other off. They were so greedy that they were plastered with more dough than they ate. First one hen and then the other slipped and fell. The sticky dough acted like a trap and their squawks were muffled by the dough on their beaks.

Nothing muffled the other chickens! The yeasty fragrance of the dough excited them. Several hens flew to the top of the out-oven, trying to get at the dough, too.

"Shoo! Shoo!" screamed Jonathan, jumping up and down, waving his arms.

Brushing and kicking chickens to right and left out of her way, Sarah Jane snatched the two hens and the rooster out of the dough and flung them to the ground. Wobbling crazily, they ran to the chicken yard, followed by all the others.

Quickly Sarah Jane lifted the gate and fastened it in place. All the chickens were shut in again. At least one of the day's problems was solved, even if it was at the cost of the bread.

But Sarah Jane did not rejoice long. She saw with horror that the dough-plastered chickens were being pecked by the others until the poor birds were stripped almost naked. The disheveled hens huddled in the farthest corner of the yard. The cock that she had once called Satan stretched his neck to crow, but his dilapidated state must have embarrassed him for he only croaked uncertainly.

"Are they dead? Will they die?" Jonathan's questions recalled his sister to her responsibilities.

"They do look bad," she said, shaking her head. "We'll have to let Pa decide what to do about them."

Picking up the bread pan, now almost empty, she started back to the house. Her brother trailed after her, looking forlorn. His unhappy face capped the other failures of the day. How had she ever dared to dream that she alone could make a good home for Pa and Jonny in Wisconsin? Again she felt more like a child than a girl of thirteen.

"Here, Jonny," she said as she handed him a little basket. "You pick up all the chips you find around the chopping block. I'm going to find out how to make biscuits to take the place of the bread those naughty old chickens spoiled. If you find enough chips for kindling we'll make the fire in the oven and have supper ready in time for Pa."

Jonathan responded to her voice which sounded more cheerful than she felt. He ran happily about the yard collecting chips while Sarah Jane went inside to relate the latest catastrophe to her stepmother.

She found Rebecca looking better. She laughed when Sarah Jane described the greedy hens to her and patted her hand. "More than that to kill those chickens," she said. "Please, don't worry."

Sarah Jane offered Rebecca a cool drink of water. Then as she dictated the correct portions of ingredients, Sarah Jane measured out the flour, salt, baking soda, lard, and water to make biscuits. She tried to heed the warning, "Handle— so very little— or bread will be tough." But

115

her fingers were caked with dough and her arms floured to the elbows before the biscuits were cut and ready to put in the out-oven. She wondered if her biscuits would be too tough to eat.

Edward Horner drove up the lane. After finding Rebecca apparently without fever and napping, he went directly to the barn to milk the cow. While he strained the milk, Sarah Jane set the table and took the biscuits from the oven. She was happy to see they had risen as well as Rebecca's biscuits.

Settling comfortably at the table, Pa buttered biscuits and told about his successful trip to Oshkosh. Rebecca was awake and smiled to watch him munch hungrily, buttering another as soon as he had finished one biscuit.

"Jonny told me the chickens spoiled your bread, Sairy," he said. "And lost a feather or two to pay for their mischief. Don't let them worry you. They'll grow new feathers and do more mischief no doubt before they find their way to the pot."

Sarah Jane relaxed only to stiffen suddenly as her father started to frown. "I told you not to let Becky do any work today," he said sternly.

"But I didn't let her do anything," Sarah Jane protested.

"Then how did she make a batch of her good biscuits?" Edward Horner demanded.

Before Sarah Jane could answer, Rebecca's low laugh sounded from the bed. "Those—they are Sarah Jane's good biscuits," Rebecca told her husband. "In my bed I rest all the day."

With a pleased smile, Edward Horner crossed the

room to hug Sarah Jane. "They are as good as Rebecca's. I declare they are. Not many women can make biscuits as good as Becky's—but you're one of those women, bless you!"

Her father's praise echoed in Sarah Jane's ears as she put Jonathan to bed and tidied the room for the night. And his praise gave wings to her tired feet as she climbed the ladder to her own bed.

Her day had not been a total failure after all.

12 *A Harvest Song*

THE WORRY on her father's face was like a threatening cloud over everything Sarah Jane did in the days that followed. Rebecca was weak and tired after the fever. Only Jonathan was as bright and lively as ever.

The garden was dry and dusty. One hot day followed another. England had not prepared Sarah Jane for an American autumn. She returned to school, but she felt uneasy.

Then one night a thunderstorm crashed and roared for hours. Each bolt of lightning seemed aimed right at the cabin. Sarah Jane woke, trembling. When the thunder receded into the distance, a downpour of rain came. Lulled by its drumming on the roof close over her head, Sarah Jane fell asleep.

In the morning there was a new briskness in the air. As she leaned out of the window to breathe deeply of the freshness the cock flew to the roof of the chicken house, flapped his wings, and crowed noisily. He had been quiet and subdued since his adventure in the dough, but now, with his feathers grown out again, he considered himself once more the lord of creation.

With each brisk night color appeared in the trees. First came the golden yellow of the elms; the flaming red of the maples came a little later. Flashing scarlet splashed across the pastures where sumac grew. Autumn in Wisconsin, vivid and bracing, was different from anything Sarah Jane had ever experienced.

One night a heavy frost came. Rebecca's flowers drooped in the morning. As the sun licked the frost from the grass, the garden rows stood black and wilted.

"Lessons will have to wait this week," her father said at breakfast. "We'll all work to get the vegetables in. Winter may break any day. When you get things well under way I must make a trip to Oshkosh to sell what we can spare."

Before she washed the breakfast dishes and attended to her bread, Rebecca showed Sarah Jane and Jonathan how to pull up the root vegetables. Sarah Jane could soon judge how deep to thrust the shovel to bring potatoes up out of the hill so that Jonathan could gather them into the basket.

Turnips and beets, carrots and parsnips, had to be grasped with just the proper firmness or the vegetables were lost. Later Sarah Jane pulled the dry bean vines and piled them in the barn to shell another time.

The next day Sarah Jane and Jonathan worked down the onion rows, building a mountain of yellow skinned onions. Rebecca knelt beside her herb bed, carefully tying bunches of thyme, tansy, rosemary, mint, and parsley.

On the morning when most of the garden rows were empty, Edward Horner caught chickens, tied their feet together, and secured them in the wagon bed. The chickens caused him some trouble in their capture, but cornering the fattest pig was more of an ordeal. After much pig squealing and Horner muttering, the pig was added to the protesting chickens in the wagon. Then came baskets of the biggest potatoes and turnips, bunches of the best carrots and parsnips, and a basket of onions. With the wagon loaded, he drove away to Oshkosh.

When he had disappeared around the bend into the elm woods, Rebecca showed the children how to knot the onions by their dry tops to hang on the rafters of the attic along with the herbs.

Sarah Jane knew by the way Jonathan's feet dragged that his body ached as hers did. She felt tired through and through. But he slapped his hands together to shake off the garden soil which still clung to them and his eyes sparkled as he said, "I'm a farmer. Are you a farmer, Sar' Jane?"

Sarah Jane dipped fresh water into the washbasin before she answered. "No, Jonny, I'm not a farmer. I think I'd like to be a schoolteacher like Miss Wallace some day or maybe write books, if I study hard enough. I'm not a farmer, Jonny. I—I hate farming. I hate it!"

The moment after her outburst Sarah Jane was ashamed as she saw Jonathan's eyes widen. He stepped slowly back and said, "Oh, no, Sar' Jane. Mummy-Becky says we are all good farmers."

That seemed the thing that was too much. "Don't say Mummy-Becky to me again!" she cried. "Don't. She's not my mother!"

Sarah Jane threw the washcloth into the basin, turned from Jonathan, and stumbled up the steps into the house. She brushed past her stepmother and climbed the ladder to her attic refuge. She breathed deeply, fighting for self-control. She must have a serene face when she went back downstairs. She must not cause distress to grow again in Jonny's eyes.

Supper was ready and waiting long before Pa returned from Oshkosh. He carried the newspaper and two small packages which he placed on the chest beside the bed. Smiling wearily, he shook his head at Jonathan who bounced up and down beside him, begging, "Let me see. Let me see!"

"Not until after supper," his father answered.

Everyone was tired and serious at the supper table—everyone but Jonathan. He had forgotten Sarah Jane's outburst, and he was too young to realize how dangerously small their harvest was. He attacked his food with his spoon before the echo of the amen to Pa's grace had faded. As Jonathan ate noisily, Sarah Jane watched him, thinking of the little boy who had been punished so often at the orphanage for not clearing his plate.

Sarah Jane slumped, picking at her food. She sighed, so large and self-pitying a sigh that her father looked at her.

"Sit up, Sarah Jane," he said sharply. "Your mamma has been up since before the sun, yet her elbows are down and her back is straight. Sit up!"

Sarah Jane straightened stiffly, her elbows tightly pressed to her sides. She leaned across the table to aim her words, like sharp little pellets of sound, directly at her father. Anger burned in her.

"My mother is in her grave in England!" she exclaimed. Then unable to trust her voice, she mechanically picked up her spoon and tried to eat.

121

"Why, you impudent child!" Her father choked and stopped.

Sarah Jane felt eyes upon her—her father's eyes angry, Jonathan's frightened and puzzled. She could not bear to look at her stepmother to read the expression on her face. She kept putting food into her mouth, but she was not sure she could swallow any of it.

It was Rebecca's voice that broke the uneasy stillness, "Edward, Edward. Her mother is in her grave in England ... It is not how I sit, not how I do. It is because her mother was dainty Sarah Jane must not slump."

Sarah Jane gasped and raised her eyes to look directly into her stepmother's. They were not angry eyes, but so kind and understanding that Sarah Jane's eyes filled with tears.

"How did you know?" she asked huskily. "You never knew her."

Rebecca shook her head. "I know partly because of the little picture. Partly because Jonathan is small and dainty. Partly because you are lovely. Sarah Jane, do not make her ashamed of you."

The earnest words were so free of anger that Sarah Jane was completely unprepared for them. She could have borne a scolding with stubborn uptilted chin. But Rebecca's words took her by surprise. She hid her face on the table, unable to control her sobs.

Pa's stool fell on the floor with a thump. Sarah Jane shivered, expecting a rough shake. Instead she felt his hand placed gently on her shoulder. "Forgive me, Sairy," he said quietly.

Sarah Jane could not speak. Everyone was silent.

The fire snapping and Jonathan's squirming uneasily in his chair were the only sounds in the room.

Then Jonathan, his voice wistful, broke the tension. "Don't we get our surprise from Oshkosh?"

Now it was Rebecca's stool which thumped to the floor as she stood suddenly. "Poor lamb!" she exclaimed. "He waits and puzzles—and waits, and waiting comes not easy to little ones."

Working quickly, she cleared the table and washed the dishes. Then Edward Horner brought from behind the bed curtain the two packages and Jonathan bounced in excitement.

"Quick! Open them so we can see," he urged.

With a flourish, Pa revealed two red-and-white striped candy canes. "One for you and one for your sister."

"Oh—oh—oh!" exclaimed Jonathan.

"Thank you, Pa," Sarah Jane said through the ache in her throat. "Jonny's never had a candy cane, and neither have I."

Jonathan licked his candy cane joyfully until Rebecca cautioned, "Only part tonight. Save for tomorrow."

Sarah Jane left her candy untouched on the table before her. She wished she could escape to bed, but Jonathan held her hand, squeezing it in his excitement. She watched the second small package which her father was unwrapping. Four cello strings uncoiled on the table. Happy memories stirred in Sarah Jane's mind.

Again Edward Horner disappeared behind the bed curtain and pulled out from under the bed something awkward and blanket wrapped. Jonathan watched, puzzled, as Pa laid aside the blanket and brought out the big fiddle. His hands were shaking with excitement as he put the four strings on the instrument. Jonathan continued to stare. He had never heard his father make music with the cello. The farm kept Pa too busy.

Pa smiled at Sarah Jane as he sat in the straight chair, the cello between his knees. Suddenly the tension between them broke. She smiled back at him, remembering the happy times in England.

Edward Horner drew the bow across the strings. They were out of tune. He grimaced and tuned the strings to his satisfaction. Then he played, the melody growing in assurance with each stroke of the bow.

Sarah Jane closed her eyes as the mellow tones filled the room, tones which she had heard last as she cuddled in Mother's arms before the hearth in Grandmum's cottage in Lincolnshire.

When Pa paused, Jonathan capered around and around the table. "Oh, goody, goody! Play us another song, Pa."

Edward Horner lifted the bow again. He played fumblingly at first. Slow, solemn hymn tunes, "Praise God From Whom All Blessings Flow," "Oh, God Our Help in Ages Past." Sometimes the tune died away uncertainly, but when he found one which he could complete, he played it over and over, each time more firmly and truly.

Sometimes when he faltered Rebecca caught the tune and sang with the cello and then a phrase ahead, until he could pick it out again. Then they would do it again for the joy of doing it together.

Without much trouble Edward Horner picked out "Believe Me, If All Those Endearing Young Charms." He played it over again, smiling at his wife as he did so. After that came "Drink to Me Only with Thine Eyes" and "My Heart's in the Highland" and "Sweet and Low."

Jonathan suddenly ran to Rebecca as if overcome by the waves of sound. Without hesitating in the melody she was singing she took the little boy on her lap.

Both Rebecca and the cello were still a moment. Edward Horner spoke, "Remember, Becky, that song you sang to me the night you nursed me through the worst of the fever? I'd like to try that, and then we'll have to stop for the night."

Without hesitation, Rebecca sang, but the words were Welsh. Her husband listened until she had finished, and then she sang it again more slowly while he groped to play the melody.

Jonathan reached up to pat Rebecca's cheek, saying "So pretty, Mummy-Becky. Now sing it with our words."

Pa stopped playing and smiled, nodding.

"I'm— I'm so stupid— I know them not," Rebecca faltered.

"Our mother sang it to us, too." Sarah Jane said, knowing now why it had roused her. "At night before she tucked us in."

"In our words?" asked Jonathan, sitting up on Rebecca's lap.

"Of course."

"Then teach them to Mummy-Becky," Jonathan ordered.

"Sing it, Sairy, can't you?" her father asked softly.

Haltingly, aware of her inability to carry a tune, Sarah Jane chanted more than sang. Word by word, it came back, fitting to the rhythm even though she could not always bring out the right tune.

> Sleep, my love, and peace attend thee
>> All through the night.
> Guardian angels God will lend thee
>> All through the night.
> Soft the drowsy hours are creeping
> Hill and vale in slumber steeping.
> I, my love, am vigil keeping
>> All through the night.

They sat silently for a few moments, and then all at once everyone jumped up to attend to the night duties. Humming the melody, Pa put the cello back in its blanket. Lending Jonathan a helping hand as he sleepily undressed, Rebecca sang it softly with Welsh and English words mingled.

As Sarah Jane started up the ladder, Rebecca crossed the room toward her, singing in English, "Sleep my love and— and what says it then?"

"And peace attend thee," Sarah Jane supplied the English words, singing them softly.

As Sarah Jane climbed into the attic, Rebecca stood at the foot of the ladder. She sang the whole line in English, "Sleep, my love, and peace attend thee, all through the night."

 13 *The Storm*

AFTER HARVEST came a quiet interval when Sarah Jane settled down to a happy routine at school. But in Wisconsin, autumn can swiftly change to winter.

The new season seemed to come silently, all in one night. Sarah Jane awoke to find a little snowdrift on the foot of her bed. She stared in disbelief from the snowdrift to the pinprick of a hole in the roof. Her fingers were numb, her nose was stiff. When she forced herself out of bed her shivering made it hard to dress.

All that day it grew colder and colder. Snow blew around the cabin. Next morning when Sarah Jane backed down the ladder into the warmth below she found her stepmother at the table. She was working on a row of plucked chickens. Jonathan, wrapped in a comforter, rocked before the fireplace in Rebecca's chair.

At that moment Pa stamped in the door, bringing bitter cold air with him. He forced the door shut against wind and swirling snow. He put down the milk pail and shook snow from his coat. He looked into the milk pail a moment and exclaimed, "The milk froze just while I was feeding the animals!"

Sarah Jane crossed the room to stare at the frozen milk. Coldness like that she had never felt before.

Murmuring in dismay, Rebecca took the pail from her husband.

Thinking about her glimpse of snowy wildness over her father's shoulder before he had forced the door shut, Sarah Jane asked, "What about school?"

"There's nobody'd be foolish enough to start out for school today," her father said. "This storm blew in shortly after midnight, and by schooltime it's only a guess as to where the road might be. You'll have to satisfy yourself with being a homebody today."

Rebecca patted butter on Sarah Jane's bowl of porridge to take the place of milk.

"It should be a cozy day," Pa said, "with all of us doing odds and ends of things in front of the fireplace. I can mend some tools and read my newspaper on such a day as this."

Clumsily with mittened hands he lifted the dressed chickens. He stepped out into the storm. Rebecca went to the north window. She blew on the thick ice on the windowpane and scraped, trying to make a peephole through which she could watch her husband's progress through the storm to the springhouse.

"Nothing—nothing but snow," she said anxiously.

Sarah Jane went to stand beside her stepmother. "Why did Pa kill them all at once this morning when the storm is making extra work?" she asked.

"Because of the storm, just because of the storm," Rebecca told her. "The chickens were frozen on their perches when he went to feed them."

"Oh, how dreadful!" Sarah Jane exclaimed.

"Shh," Rebecca warned softly, "we'll not upset

Jonathan."

Sarah Jane looked quickly over her shoulder at her brother. He was rocking happily before the fire, snuggled in the comforter.

"We dressed them quickly to save them—food will be scarce this winter with the pigs all going to market to pay the debt," Rebecca said. She scraped again at the peephole.

Winter like that—freezing chickens on their perches, freezing away the view from a window, freezing milk in its pail—was not just another season of the year, colder and less agreeable as it had been in England. It was cruel and ruthless.

"Pa's been gone a long time," Sarah Jane ventured. "And it's so cold. Is he all right?"

Rebecca laid a finger quickly across Sarah Jane's lips, but she nodded. "Too long. I—I think we should call for him. You stay with Jonny."

Rebecca took a heavy cloak from the hook.

"No, please, you mustn't go out," Sarah Jane said more loudly than she intended. Jonathan stopped rocking and turned to look at them.

"Hush!" Rebecca said, gesturing toward Jonathan. "I only stand for a moment on the steps and call. My voice will be a beacon for Edward."

Sarah Jane hurried to Jonathan, turning the chair so that its back was toward the door. "This way," she told him. "Back to the wind and face the fire. Isn't that better, Jonny?"

"Edward! Edward! Edward!" came Rebecca's voice, faint in the shriek of the wind.

Sarah Jane held her breath straining to hear an answering shout. There was nothing—nothing but the howl of the wind.

Rebecca's dark hair was frosted with snow when she came in, panting. She tossed cloak, mittens, and shawl over the chair and hurried to the chest at the end of the big bed. Throwing it open, she laid aside carefully stacked garments until she found a coil of rope.

"No answer," she said desperately. "We must go after him. You are more sure of foot than I. Put on all the warm things. Then I tie this to your waist. Go as far as it lets you—every direction before you return. You need help—tug it three times. I will follow the rope to you."

Rebbeca knotted an end of the rope around Sarah Jane's waist and gave her the coil. She looped the other end around her own wrist. At the door she held Sarah Jane a moment before letting her go.

"The springhouse first," she said. She gave Sarah Jane's arm a last squeeze. "Remember, three hard tugs for help."

Sarah Jane stood alone then in the wild wind and snow. The cold nipped her nostrils shut. The wind snatched away her breath. She drew her scarf across her nose and mouth. Breathing was easier then, and she stepped away from the door, thinking how much harder it must be for Pa who had been out longer.

Slowly she followed the north wall of the house toward the springhouse. She could see nothing through the whirling storm. Pellets of wind-driven snow stung her face. She closed her eyes and guided herself by one hand against the wall of the cabin. When she stepped beyond the wall, the full force of the wind struck her. She slipped and floundered in the deep snow. She paused for a moment, swaying in the wind.

"Father! Father! Pa!" she called. She waited, but there was no anwser. She pushed on. The shadow looming before her must be the springhouse. She stumbled against it and fumbled for the door. It opened suddenly and she fell to her knees. She crawled forward into the protection and quiet of the springhouse. She leaned against the wall, breathing heavily.

"Pa, are you here?" she called. But she knew from the empty stillness that she was alone in the springhouse. She groped along the length of the little room just to make sure he was not there, frozen and helpless. The chickens he had brought hung from the rafters, but he was not there.

When she was outside again she walked step by step, breath by weary breath. She turned toward the barn first. Perhaps he went there if he had missed the house.

Once she fell into a snowdrift. She thought that she could never get up again. She was tangled in the rope when she tried to stand. She hoped her stepmother would not think she was calling for help. She was no longer dignified Sarah Jane, too proud to cry; she was weakness pitted against cruel force. When she was on her feet again, she turned for a moment to rest with her back to the wind. "Pa? Pa?" she called while she rested. There was no answer to her call. She forced her way on.

Suddenly the wind attacked her from a new angle and slammed her against a solid log wall. She had found the barn.

"Pa, Pa?" she screamed as she felt her way along the wall, groping for the door. "Pa? Can you hear me? Are you in here?"

Then she fell again, headfirst into the windswept snow. As she struggled to her feet she realized that she had been moving along the doorless south wall of the barn. She went on toward the place where the door should be—and there it was!

"Pa?" she called, pounding the door. There was no answer and she could not move the heavy door. Snow was drifted so high against it that she decided her father had not been there since he had brought in the milk.

Sarah Jane leaned against the door, gasping and sobbing. From the moment she had left the springhouse she had been hoping, hoping she would find her father safe in the barn. She took a deep breath and plunged on.

Turning a shoulder to the blast of the wind so that she should be going east toward the road, she went step by step, wearily, so wearily. After each three steps she stopped to rest. Before going on she called, "Pa, Pa!"

Then she reached the end of the rope. Trying not to panic, she started what she hoped was a wide circle just within the limit of the rope. Step, step, step, rest. Then the call into the shrieking wind, "Pa, Pa!"

She started back toward the house. Step, step, step, rest. She had no more breath to call. She started on and fell over something—something that stirred and moaned. She had found her father!

He struggled and rose to his knees. "Sairy!" he said hoarsely. "Sairy, what .. are .. you .. doing .. out .. here?"

"To get you, I came to get you. You took so long."

"Child!" His teeth were chattering so hard he could not say more for a moment. Sarah Jane helped him to his feet. "Child, you should . . not be . . out . . in this storm. I've lost my way . . dizzy in the snow. . . ."

Sarah Jane tugged at her father's arm. "Let's get back to the house she said through chattering teeth. Her father seemed dangerously dazed.

They moved slowly. Fear shook Sarah Jane as fiercely as the wind did. Her rhythm of three steps and a rest was too much for Pa. They stumbled and almost fell, but Sarah Jane held tightly to his arm and succeeded in getting him to his feet again.

Sarah Jane urged her father ahead, one step, one step, one step. At last the cabin wall loomed before them and they were protected from the force of the wind. They were near enough for Rebecca to hear Sarah Jane's voice urging her father forward.

Rebecca met them. She placed one arm around Edward. Sarah Jane pushed, and at last they got him into the cabin.

While Rebecca tucked her husband into the bed with comforters piled on him and bricks heated at the hearth against his feet, Jonathan pushed Sarah Jane into the rocker before the fire.

"Poor, poor Sar' Jane," he crooned, draping his comforter around her. "Lost in the cold. My poor Sar' Jane. I'm a big boy now. I take care of you."

When at last father and daughter no longer shivered, Rebecca rubbed their frostbitten cheeks and noses with snow. Then she fed them broth. The whole day seemed spent in recapturing warmth. And then it was time to go to the barn to care for the animals for the night.

The wind howled as cruelly as ever. The house itself shuddered. Pellets of snow swept against the windowpane. "Don't go out again," Sarah Jane pleaded.

"Daughter, we can't risk the loss of any more of our animals," her father told her.

"And there'll be no more getting lost for you," Rebecca said briskly. She handed her husband the rope. "This you tie from house to barn," she directed, and he obeyed.

Sarah Jane, who had been rocking cozily before the fire with Jonathan beside her, sat quietly, straining for sound of Pa. Jonathan wiggled out of the rocker and went to the window to scratch a new peephole. At last he shouted, "Here he is! Pa is not lost."

Edward Horner put the milk pail on the table. He shook his head. "Seems as if the wind's going to starve us if it can't freeze me."

Sarah Jane looked into the pail. It was barely one third full. She asked, "What was the matter with Daisy?"

"Nothing's the matter with Daisy," Pa said. "That pail was full when I left the barn. Wind snatched most of it away."

"Never mind. We are all safe," Rebecca said. "And it's enough for hot milk and bread before bed. What more can we ask tonight?"

As soon as they had eaten, Rebecca went about getting the room ready for the night. Sarah Jane slept on a bench in the kitchen corner. The attic was too cold. Before she fell asleep she noticed that the wind no longer raged.

"I'm glad the storm has stopped," she thought sleepily. "Perhaps I can go to school tomorrow."

When daylight came, they found that the storm was not over—only the wind had ceased its blustering. Snow fell that day, a thick curtain of it that obscured everything. It fell that night and all the next day. A day was not measured by the position of the sun in the sky but by Pa's labored trips to the barn to care for the animals.

Sarah Jane darned socks. Jonathan wound yarn into a big ball for Rebecca. Pa read slowly aloud from the Democrat, and Sarah Jane studied her spelling words for three lessons ahead until she was sure she could spell every word forward and backward. At the end of the day Pa brought out the cello and they sang before bedtime.

On the fourth morning the sky was clear. The rising sun turned the world into a brilliant place of shapes and forms they had never seen before. They could only guess where the lane ran to the road. Fence posts were entirely hidden. The springhouse was buried in a mighty drift.

They spent two days digging tunnels and paths to barn, woodpile, springhouse, and slowly down the lane to the county road. On Monday morning when Thomas Hughes paused at the end of the lane with a sleigh full of laughing, singing children Sarah Jane ran to join them on a well packed path between walls of snow piled almost as high as her head.

14 *Wintry Days*

SARAH JANE worked hard each day at school. If she could learn every word in the spelling book, every fact about the world in the geography book, every example in the arithmetic book, then she would be wise enough to go away to earn her own living. For Sarah Jane still had a secret plan.

As soon as she had given Pa enough help to repay him for the expense of bringing her to America, she would go. She knew now that she must go alone, but she felt confident she could do it. Jonathan was happy and healthy with Pa and their stepmother. But life on the farm was a constant struggle. And she could not free her mind of the conviction formed on that July day when she first learned about her stepmother. For her to remain in Rebecca's home was to be disloyal to her own mother, to be a burden to her father.

Often as Sarah Jane watched her stepmother's efficient, quiet management of the home she wondered why her father was so insistent that he needed his daughter's help, slow and awkward as she often was. He seemed to guard Rebecca, often watching her when she did not notice.

"Why is Pa so worried?" Sarah Jane wondered. Since recovering from the chills and fever Rebecca Horner was the rosy cheeked picture of health. "It must be because our mother died," Sarah Jane decided.

Feeling uneasy and eager to be out on her own, Sarah Jane was impatient with every interruption at school. But the weather was against her. Through November and into December, storms howled so wildly that there was no school for days at a time.

The third week of December by some wonder was storm free, at least until Friday afternoon. Then the schoolroom darkened and the building seemed to shudder as the wind suddenly roared against it from the northwest. Sleet rattled against the windows. As Miss Wallace gave out spelling words for the Friday spelling match her eyes strayed to the window. When the last speller had missed and been spelled down, Miss Wallace piled wood into the stove and read aloud to the children Mr. Hawthorne's new story, "The Great Stone Face," even though it was time to ring the handbell to end the schoolday.

It grew dark as night and the lamp which Miss Wallace lighted on her desk cast too little light for schoolwork. Clapping her hands, Miss Wallace started to sing—nursery rhymes, counting songs, psalms—and the children joined her.

Sarah Jane's stomach was tightening with hunger and others too thought of food. In the silence between songs, the wind roared and little Lucy May Watson started to whimper. Henry tried to hush her, shaking her impatiently. She pulled away from her brother and ran to Sarah Jane. "I'm hungry," she wailed as Sarah Jane lifted her to her lap.

Miss Wallace opened the top drawer of her desk. She took out a paper bag. "I was saving this for an end-of-the-term treat," she said. "But I think popcorn on a cold winter afternoon is much better, don't you?"

She lifted the popcorn popper, a rectangular screen basket with a long handle, from the shelf in the corner. The boys and girls left their seats to crowd around the stove. The room filled with chatter punctuated by the staccato popping of the corn.

One of the Darwin boys sheepishly emptied his pockets to make a pile of black walnuts on the floor beside the stove. With a stone for a hammer he cracked the nuts.

Myrtie took from the corner of her desk three winter apples and offered, "We could divide these four ways and twelve of us could have a taste."

Following Myrtie's lead, several other girls placed apples on the teacher's desk. Then two cookies appeared, two doughnuts, a piece of applesauce cake, and a wedge of cheese, all leftovers from lunch baskets.

The pan which Miss Wallace took down from the shelf in the corner was filled with popcorn. The nuts, cake, apples, and cheese were divided. Everyone munched and laughter drowned the sounds of the storm.

As soon as Sarah Jane had eaten her share she turned to her desk. She worried, were Jonathan and Rebecca and Pa safe? The wind was no longer blowing and she tiptoed to the window to breathe a peephole in a heavily frosted pane. As she put her eye close to the hole the out-of-doors grew brighter. Through ragged clouds in the west the sun was sinking below the horizon —sunset! Only four o'clock! Sarah Jane was surprised because she had thought it was much later. The sleet had changed to snow. Would they perhaps have to stay at school all night?

She turned as Miss Wallace put another chunk of wood in the stove. Brushing slivers and bark dust from her hands, the teacher came to stand beside Sarah Jane.

"It has started to snow," Sarah Jane said softly.

"I thought as much when the wind went down," Miss Wallace answered.

Fearing what the night threatened, Sarah Jane said under her breath, "We daren't walk home in this storm. What if we don't have enough wood?"

Miss Wallace smiled and shook her gently by the arm. "Evanses, across the road, won't let us freeze, silly girl."

"Their house won't hold us all," Sarah Jane objected.

"But they've a good pile of wood," Miss Wallace said. "And they are not the kind of folks to see anyone go cold, least of all at the school where their own children go."

Remembering how her own father had nearly been lost in the snow close to the cabin, she said, "But in the storm you can get lost just trying to go to the woodpile."

"Sarah, Sarah!" Miss Wallace put her arm around the girl's waist. "Do you know what you have to learn more than anything I can teach you in books? You must learn to stop worrying. You're too young to frown like that. Learn to take life as it comes. Worrying is such a waste of time and strength, and we always worry about the wrong thing anyway. Subtract incorrectly. Add shakily for a while longer. Forget the spelling words. Let it all go and I'll call you my prize scholar for the year if you just learn to stop worrying."

What a strange thing for a teacher to say! How different from anything Sarah Jane had heard from Matron at the orphanage. She was staring at Miss Wallace when the sound of sleigh bells brought everyone rushing to the windows.

Eliza Hughes called excitedly, "Those are my father's sleigh bells. He's come to take us home!"

"You see," Miss Wallace whispered to Sarah Jane in the hubbub, "we always worry about the wrong thing."

Thomas Hughes joined the children at the stove. They made room for him to warm his hands and offered what was left of the popcorn. He scooped up a big handful and munched hungrily. Then he turned to Miss Wallace.

"I'll take all of them that live around the south edge of the marsh on this trip," he said. "And then I'll circle around the marsh after I leave the Baxters and pick up those that go north on the Oshkosh Road. I'll carry a chunk or two from the Evanses' woodpile to keep you warm until I get back."

The sleigh sped along the snowy road and up the Horner lane. The door of the cabin swung open and Pa appeared to lift Sarah Jane from the sleigh. Her father's face seemed haunted by anxiety. Miss Wallace's cheerful banishment of worry faded as the winter evening wore on.

When Jonathan was asleep in the trundle bed and Sarah Jane was settled for the night on the bench before the fireplace, she heard her father and stepmother talking softly. The tone of her stepmother's voice brought Sarah Jane wide awake. She knew she should not be listening but stillness outdoors and the quiet in the cabin made even whispered words audible.

"I hate to tell you, Edward . . . the flour barrel . . . it is . . . empty. It was the last bread today. Now only a day or two . . . and the meal . . . gone."

Pa blew out the candle and the cornhusks in the mattress rustled. There was a long silence before her father's answer.

"I noticed. And in the springhouse there's only one small piece of side meat. I'll take a dollar or two from the savings and go to Oshkosh for supplies as soon as the chores are finished in the morning. You'll be all right for the day."

Sarah Jane could not understand Rebecca's words, but the protest in her tone was clear.

"Only a dollar or two," her father repeated, "enough to get a bit of salt pork and meal and flour to carry us until the weather eases. Then I'll see if I can get work by the day, hauling or woodcutting or something, enough to get cash money in the pocket."

"Thomas would help," Rebecca suggested.

"Not one cent more from Thomas!" Pa's voice was angry.

"Shh, shh," Rebecca warned. "Thomas always would help—"

Pa's voice was softer but still determined. "It's been

a hard winter for us all. And since the wolves broke into Thomas's smokehouse, well, it's not going to be easy for them before the winter's over. No, I'm going to Oshkosh tomorrow as soon as the chores are done. Thomas told me he was going and I'll go with him. My hands are quick and strong, Becky, if I can just find work for them."

All was still on the other side of the curtain. Sarah Jane wished there were weaving or some other such occupation for her father in this new land. In the distance she heard the howl of wolves. They were hungry, too, in the deep snow. The animals were coming closer to the settlement than they had in years, so the old settlers were saying. Sarah Jane shivered, but the warm blanket of sleep was stronger this time than the cold howl of hunger and she slept.

15 *A New Face*

BEFORE SARAH JANE had her boots buttoned next morning, sleigh bells sounded and horses whinnied in the lane. Edward Horner stamped in, followed by Thomas Hughes, Martha, his quiet wife, and little Owen who was the same age as Jonathan.

"Owen wants to ride into town with his papa," Martha Hughes explained. "Jonathan will have fun, too, and if you go to keep an eye on them, Sarah Jane, the two men will make short work of laying in provisions to see us through the storm that's gathering."

Sarah Jane looked from her father to her stepmother, surprised at the unexpected turn in events. Rebecca looked tired and moved clumsily as she worked at the table, putting cold meat between slices of cornbread to make a lunch.

Her father evaded Sarah Jane's questioning glance as he helped Jonathan into his coat and bundled an extra scarf across the little boy's face.

Rebecca crossed the room and drew from the fireplace several bricks which had been warming near the flames.

"Step lively, daughter," Edward Horner said. "These bricks won't do you much good as footwarmers in the sleigh if you let them cool off before we get started."

He held Sarah Jane's cloak for her. Reluctantly Sarah Jane pulled it about her. A trip to Oshkosh in the cold did not seem so inviting to her.

"Where's Eliza?" she asked Martha Hughes, as she accepted the wrapped bricks from her.

"Keeping the home fires burning for me, keeping an eye on the boys, and teaching her sister to knit a sock," Martha Hughes answered with a laugh. She seemed to be pushing Sarah Jane toward the door.

"Shouldn't I stay and help here?" Sarah Jane protested.

"Rebecca and I will do nicely," Martha Hughes said, opening the door. "But I can't say the same for the men in town if they have to look after Jonny and Owen all day. Run along now, they need you. And smile and have a good time, too."

Laughing together, Owen and Jonathan let themselves be picked up by Thomas Hughes and tucked into the straw in the sleigh, along with the heated bricks and a mound of blankets and comforters.

With a helping hand from her father, Sarah Jane climbed into the sleigh and nestled into the straw with the two little boys. Thomas Hughes handed her Martha's little footwarmer. After a final rearrangement of the blankets around the children, he jumped into the sleigh beside Edward Horner. They were off into the force of the north wind, sleigh bells pealing melodiously.

Jonathan and Owen, snug in the blankets, were singing and laughing together. Over the happy murmur of their voices Sarah Jane heard Thomas Hughes speak to her father.

"Stop worrying, Ed. Rebecca's as strong and hearty as they come."

"A man can't help worrying," her father answered, shifting the scarf across his mouth and nose. "And there's the worry of having to take help from you. A man ought to be able to feed his own family. You've given us too much already."

Thomas Hughes only growled in answer and settled more deeply into his coat collar and scarf. There was nothing more to hear from the seat above, nothing more for Sarah Jane to do but snuggle into the straw and wonder and worry.

The riders were stiff with cold when finally they swept across the bridge into Oshkosh and up Ferry Street. They stopped before Smith's Corner Grocery. The children hurried inside on numb feet and stood shivering around the stove in the store, eating the pieces of cornbread and cold meat Rebecca had packed for them. Edward Horner and Thomas Hughes argued over purchases at the front counter.

Then while Thomas Hughes and Owen hurried up the street to Uncle David's house behind the Welsh church to leave socks and scarf and mittens Eliza and Martha had knitted for him, Sarah Jane and Jonathan followed their father across the street and up the stairs to the newspaper office.

Sarah Jane shrank shyly from the noisy greeting of Mr. Burnside, the editor, and the curious eyes of the two apprentice boys whom she remembered from her summer visit in the newspaper office. Jonathan was at home at once, shaking hands with Mr. Burnside, eagerly accepting

145

the striped candy cane he offered. As Edward Horner talked with Mr. Burnside, Jonathan followed the apprentice boys asking, "What's that?" "Why are you doing that?" about everything, until Sarah Jane blushed and tried to pull him back beside her.

"That's all right," the red-headed apprentice boy assured Sarah Jane. "I have a brother just about his size."

Sarah Jane retreated to a chair beside the stove in time to hear her father's words. "Of course I like your paper, George. But there's an end to the money, and no more in sight from that poor farm. You'll have to stop sending me the paper. That's all there is to it."

"Now, I call that a real shame!" said Mr. Burnside. "You're one of the best subscribers I have, Ed."

Edward Horner shook his head. "A man that's borrowing for the food to keep his family alive—a newspaper's not for him. When work opens up in the spring, I'll look for a steady job. It seems I never was meant to be a farmer anyway. When there's money coming in again you can be sure, George, the Democrat is the first luxury I'll allow myself."

Sarah Jane felt she could cry in sympathy at the discouraged tone in Pa's voice and the tired sag of his shoulders. Mr. Burnside sat teetering his chair on the two back legs, staring at Edward Horner as if he had never seen him before. Across the room, Jonathan exclaimed excitedly over his name which the red-headed apprentice boy had just printed for him on a piece of scrap paper.

Suddenly Mr. Burnside dropped his chair noisily onto all four legs again and exclaimed loudly, "By jove, Horner! You're my man."

146

Sarah Jane turned from Jonathan to see what Mr. Burnside's exclamation meant. She could tell from the expression on Pa's face that he was as puzzled as she was.

"To take Jake's place, I mean," Mr. Burnside said. "Jake and his bottle have been getting closer and closer ever since his wife died. Last week his daughter came and took him back to Milwaukee with her. Leaves me without typesetter and handyman right in the dead of winter. On busy days there's too much for just the boys and me. I really miss old Jake. Yes, siree, Ed, you're my man."

"But—but I'm a weaver and a failure of a farmer, George," Edward Horner said. "I'm no typesetter. I'm no newspaperman."

"You want a steady job. You just said so." Mr. Burnside was on his feet, shaking Edward Horner's hand.

"Yes, but I'm a weaver by trade."

"And no weaving mills within fifty miles, and none of them wanting hand weavers," Mr. Burnside said. "Say you'll come into the Democrat office and lend me a hand. Give the work a try. What could be fairer?"

"What good will I be to you?" Edward Horner asked.

Sarah Jane heard a hopeful lift to his voice that contradicted his words.

"You can learn, man, you can learn. And you're a good man, Ed, and dependable. No drinking it up with you. What do you say, Ed?"

As the door opened and Thomas Hughes and Owen came in bringing cold air with them, Edward Horner was saying, "Why—why—I don't rightly know what to say."

"Say to what?" asked Thomas Hughes.

"Jake has left me," Mr. Burnside explained. "I'm

147

proposing to Ed, here, that he come into the office as my handyman and general helper, even to learn to set a bit of type. Ed's my man. I'm sure of it. Look at those long, slim hands. Weaver's hand and cello player's hands. Better suited to a type stick than to a plow handle I'd say."

Mr. Burnside was letting his enthusiasm carry him away. He shook Pa's hand again and slapped him on the shoulder.

Sarah Jane watched as Thomas Hughes and her father stared thoughtfully at each other. Then Thomas Hughes cleared his throat.

"It strikes me, Ed, that it's an answer to your prayers," he said.

"But I'm a weaver," Edward Horner said again, almost stubbornly.

"You were a weaver," Thomas Hughes said slowly. "You've tried your hand at farming, trying to build a better life for your family. But it strikes me for a long time now that you're no farmer, Ed, if you'll pardon me for saying so."

Sarah Jane watched her father as he flushed. She wished Uncle Thomas had not pointed out Pa's failure so bluntly.

"Yes, the more I think of it, the more I think it's an answer to your prayers. George is right. You've got the hands for skilled indoor things that I'd bungle—worse than you bungle with your hands on the plow, Ed. And this would give you a steady cash job."

Mr. Burnside slapped his thigh and laughed, highly pleased. "Well, Ed, what do you say now?"

"Why . . . why . . . I suppose . . I . . I'll say yes . . .

148

if you think I'm your man. But what am I to do with my family? I can't leave them alone on the farm in this weather. And with Becky—"

"I've the answer to that, too," exclaimed Mr. Burnside. "I own the little house Jake and his wife lived in. It sets off Ferry Street back of the Patterson place."

That description did not mean anything to Sarah Jane, listening eagerly, but both her father and Thomas Hughes nodded.

Mr. Burnside went on, "Jake was buying it from me, but he never made another payment after his wife died. I'll let you have it for the remaining two hundred, and we'll take it out of your wages each week."

They talked a few moments more. Sarah Jane watched as her father signed a paper on Mr. Burnside's desk.

Then Thomas Hughes, stooping, picked up Owen in one arm and Jonathan in the other.

"I hate to hurry such an important deal, but dark comes fast these December days, and the stock must be fed. And we want to see how Rebecca is doing and all . . ."

The cold was bitter as the sun westered in the wintry sky, and there were no warm bricks in the sleigh this time. Sarah Jane hugged the two little boys close to her and thought about the strange new turn to their lives. And having seen Jonny and Owen together all day, her thoughts for a moment hovered over what a baby brother might mean to the family. But she pushed the idea jealously away.

For half a year now, Sarah Jane realized, she had lived in the lonely, empty country. Or so it still seemed to her after her childhood in an English village and four years in the crowded city of Lincoln. Yes, she thought, she might like to return to town, even to an American town like Oshkosh. It would be easier to find the work she dreamed of getting, to find the independence she coveted. Warm now, she wondered drowsily what the changes would mean to Rebecca.

With a last peal of the sleigh bells they stopped before the cabin.

"Here we are—home, sweet Horner home!" called Uncle Thomas.

Almost before the sleigh had stopped, Edward Horner jumped from the seat and ran to the cabin. Leaving Uncle Thomas to get the little boys and the purchases out of the sleigh, Sarah Jane scrambled stiffly out and hurried after her father.

As she pushed the door open, Sarah Jane heard from the bed corner the mewling cry a tiny baby makes. Rebecca crooned one of the musical Welsh words she said in happy moments and the crying stopped.

Sarah Jane pushed the door shut and hurried across the room. Her father was bending over the bed and Rebecca was smiling up at him.

So her suspicions were true! Sarah Jane had hidden her questions about the baby clothes given to Rebecca by a woman at church. She had sought for a reason for Pa's cautions to relieve her stepmother of hard work. She had surmised what she had not put into words, had hardly shaped into thoughts. And now in this moment that brought such joy to the others she felt a stab of jealousy. Poor little Jonathan who had never been a baby in his own home!

"It's a girl, Edward," Rebecca said softly.

"Another Becky to gladden our days!" Pa said. He bent and kissed Rebecca.

With a mixture of anger and jealousy and a fresh sense of grief for her own mother, Sarah Jane turned, ready to rush out to Jonathan. Rebecca's voice stopped her.

"No, no, Edward, her name is Charity—sweet Charity Horner."

"Becky, Becky!" Edward Horner said, stubborn argument sounding in his voice. "If Rebecca is not to be her name, then wouldn't you like Bronwen, after your mother —or Mary Ann, after the little girl that's lost?"

"No, Edward. She is Charity. Jonathan's sister—and Sarah Jane's—must be Charity."

"Becky, Becky," Edward Horner said in a strange choked voice. He kissed Rebecca again.

Sarah Jane turned quickly to the door. Thomas Hughes carried Jonathan and Owen in and set them down in front of the fireplace. Sarah Jane knelt to help Jonathan unbundle. She rubbed his cheeks, red and chapped from the cold. She hugged him, and then in the feeling of relief which swept over, she kissed the tip of his cold nose and laughed happily with him. Her moment of anger, before she knew the baby was a girl, had gone completely. Jonathan was still her father's dearly beloved son. No baby boy would be nudging him aside when she, Sarah Jane, was no longer there to protect him.

Then Rebecca called Jonathan and Sarah Jane to the bed to see little Charity. The whole room was full of loving laughter and warmth and safety.

151

After a critical glance at the baby, Jonathan was more interested in Owen. Sarah Jane stood smiling at the little red face framed in long glossy black hair. Jonathan had not been so big nor so plump when he was four months old and they had gone to the orphanage. Gently Sarah Jane put her finger on the baby's hand, and the little fingers closed tightly over her finger in that convulsive, strong grip newborn babies have.

Sarah Jane wondered about the solemn and beautiful name Rebecca insisted upon giving her baby: Charity, Charity Horner.

"Come, come!" Uncle Thomas said loudly. "Night's overtaking us. Ed, come unload your provisions. We must be getting home."

In a whirl of noise and laughter the provisions were brought in from the sleigh and the Hughes family left. Pa went to the barn to milk the cow and bed down the oxen. Sarah Jane put away the meal and side meat and a roast and molasses from Oshkosh. She set the table and filled the bowls with the stew Martha Hughes had simmering in the iron kettle.

At supper, Pa let his stew grow cold as he told Rebecca about Mr. Burnside's offer of steady work and a cozy home. They made lighthearted plans for moving, with more laughter than Sarah Jane had heard in the months she had lived in the cabin.

Sarah Jane went about the evening duties in a fog of dreamy uncertainty. This day had been more full of surprises than the day Pa's letter had come with money for their passage to America.

The baby was here, a girl, no threat to Jonathan.

Soon Rebecca would be on her feet, strong and able, no longer needing help from Sarah Jane.

Then Sarah Jane could go—go somewhere to a place that would mean honor to her mother. She could be of service to Pa, too, earning money to help buy the new house. And for Jonathan there would a be a grown-up sister's help to give him whatever a little boy needs and wants. Come May and she'd be fourteen, a young lady, more than able to look after herself.

She bent over little Charity one last time before she went to bed. As she let the baby grasp her finger she laughed softly over the strength in that baby grip. She'd miss her brother when she set out to make her fortune, Sarah Jane knew. And now it came to her that it would be hard to leave this little half sister as well.

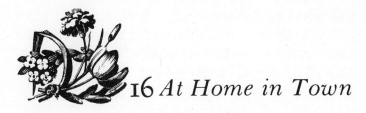

16 *At Home in Town*

SARAH JANE seemed to stand taller and stronger that week as she kept the fire going, the room tidy, the meals on time, and Jonathan busy and contented. It was almost like the dream come true: Sarah Jane making a home for her father and Jonathan.

The storm which had been gathering on the horizon the day they went to Oshkosh blew in on Charity's second day, bringing so much snow that no one went to school. Sarah Jane studied spelling words or recited states and capitals or practiced multiplication tables while she did dishes or churned. Her stepmother, regaining her strength, quietly cared for the baby or played singing games with Jonathan. She was no longer a threat to Sarah Jane's peace of mind. It was a happy week for Sarah Jane.

On Sunday, after the hour of the worship service at the little church in the Welsh community, sleigh runners squeaked outside the Horner door. Sarah Jane released the latch to welcome Hugh Edwards and Margaret, his wife, from the Welsh community. They had come to say good-bye to the Horners and make the acquaintance of Charity. Thomas and Martha Hughes had brought to church news of the baby and of the move to Oshkosh.

Before the Edwardses left, Matthew Jones and his wife, Anna, came. It was Anna, Sarah Jane remembered, who had given her stepmother the bundle of little clothes.

All day long friends came and the house was full and resounding with Welsh chatter. Following her stepmother's directions, Sarah Jane sliced the roast which had come from Oshkosh. Each woman who came during the day brought a kettle or pan to keep hot on the hearth, so though the house was full, the cupboard held more food that night than it had in the morning.

Late in the afternoon, Miss Tillie Wallace came to tell Rebecca and Sarah Jane good-bye, for she, too, had heard the news. She brought Sarah Jane's slate and slate pencil.

"You mustn't stop school just because you are moving out of our district," Miss Wallace said. "We're going to miss you. But you're too good a scholar to waste any time. Someday you could become a teacher yourself, Sarah Jane, or a writer."

"Oh, but I'm needed at home. I'll not be having time for school now that we have Charity," Sarah Jane replied.

"Nonsense!" Miss Wallace said. "Your ma isn't going to need much more help than she did before—maybe not as much in a more convenient house in town. My friend, Mrs. Bryant, has her school on Algoma Street in Oshkosh. I intend to tell her about you the next time I see her and say to expect you as one of her pupils. Get all the schooling you can, Sarah Jane. Never waste the good mind the Lord gave you."

New Year's Day, 1853! It was still dark when Pa

155

called Sarah Jane. Jonathan was already awake, bright-eyed with excitement. Charity cried hungrily. Pa hurried about, scarcely finishing one task before he started another. Only Rebecca was calm.

Pa, Jonathan, and Sarah Jane gulped breakfast standing before the fire while Rebecca fed Charity. The meal over, Rebecca directed the packing of the possessions that were to go to the new home in town.

When Thomas Hughes drove into the yards before the sun was up everything had been stowed into the old satchel or folded into blankets to make neat bundles. The furniture was packed quickly into the sleigh. Uncle Thomas was taking over the oxen, wagon, and farm tools. Daisy the cow would find a new home in his barn.

Rebecca, cuddling Charity, sat on the seat of the sleigh between her brother and her husband. Pa held the cello, swaddled in an old gray blanket. With hot bricks at their feet, Sarah Jane and Jonathan sat in the hay in the center of the sleigh, barricaded from the wind by the large pieces of furniture.

The loaded sleigh slid sedately over the snowy road, but it seemed no time at all to Sarah Jane before they were crossing the bridge into Oshkosh and moving up Ferry Street. They passed the shops, and Uncle Thomas reined the horses to a stop before a little box of a house, half logs, half unpainted boards.

Sarah Jane stood on legs so numb that they seemed to be no part of her. She climbed awkwardly from the sleigh and helped Jonathan into the new house. It was cozy, and there was the delicious smell of stew from a bowl steaming on the table set near the black cookstove.

A short plump woman in a white apron, with hair as white, put down the spoon with which she had been stirring the stew.

"Welcome! Welcome to Oshkosh," she said, bustling toward them. "I'm Esther Patterson, your next-door neighbor. When George Burnside told me you were coming in today and bringing that precious babe I told Mr. Patterson, 'Nothing like a dish of good hot stew after a long ride in the cold.'" As an afterthought she added, "Meet Mr. Patterson."

Mr. Patterson was a meek little man, as silent as his wife was talkative. He helped Edward Horner unload the furniture while Thomas Hughes joined Rebecca and Sarah Jane and Jonathan at the table for a bowl of stew.

Edward Horner ate his stew while Thomas Hughes stood with his back to the stove, drinking coffee and warming himself before the cold drive back to the farm.

The Pattersons were joined by their roomer, a big, gruff man, Dr. Howard.

"Welcome, neighbors!" the doctor said. He patted Jonathan on the head, bowed with dignity to Sarah Jane, and peeked in a professional manner at Charity, sleeping in Rebecca's arms.

Then they all left and the Horners explored the new home. They examined every nook and corner of the little house. Dingy outside, it was snug and warm and roomy inside. Across the front was the big kitchen-living room. At the back was a slant-roofed shed for wood and storage. Rebecca exclaimed in pleasure over the convenience of it. At the other end were two bedrooms.

Standing for a moment with hands on hips, Rebecca

157

surveyed the layout, her dark eyes sparkling. Then with eloquent gestures of her graceful hands making up for her lack of English words, she directed her husband in the placing of furniture and belongings. The smaller of the two bedrooms was to be for the parents, she made it clear. Charity's cradle was placed at the foot of the big bed.

Then, softly scolding herself in Welsh, Rebecca sorted through the packed bedding and linens until she found the curtain which had screened off the bedroom corner of the cabin. In her eagerness she slipped unconsciously from her broken English into Welsh, but both Sarah Jane and her father soon understood. Rebecca wanted the curtain hung the full length of the larger bedroom, dividing it into two smaller rooms, a room for Sarah Jane and a room for Jonathan.

The little boy capered in delight to have graduated from the trundle bed into a room of his own. While they were laughing at his antics, a loud knock sounded at the front door. Pa opened it, and in burst George Burnside with his hat clapped on the back of his head at a rakish angle, a fat cigar in his mouth.

Mr. Burnside bowed to Rebecca, winked at Sarah Jane, tossed Jonathan high above his head, and shook hands with Pa. "Get yourselves settled today and come on down to the Democrat office bright and early in the morning. We'll get you started. Lord knows I need you. Putting out the paper on time with only the apprentice boys to help me was like to be the death of me."

The Horner household was in an uproar next morning as Pa prepared for his first day at the new job.

"A new day. A new year. A new job, and a new

and better life," Pa declaimed.

Then he made a song of it and sang it loudly as he shaved. The mirror hung between the bedroom doors, beside the shelf holding the tintype of Jane Horner. The sound of his voice woke Charity sleeping in her cradle just beyond the door. She cried loudly.

While her stepmother fed the baby, Sarah Jane dished up the oatmeal porridge. Jonathan picked up Pa's song and pranced around the room loudly singing:

"A new day, a new year;
a new job.
A new and better life—life—life!"

Sarah Jane had a hard time capturing him to tie a towel bibwise around his neck and get him seated at his place at the table. Everyone ate without thinking about the food, for Pa's excitement infected them all.

They gathered at the door to send him off. Rebecca adjusted his scarf and kissed him. Then she watched him as he made his way to the street. Her eyes shone with her pride and love, and the red in her cheeks deepened.

Watching her stepmother, Sarah Jane thought, "She does love Pa . . . and she's beautiful that way."

And then the stab of guilt came that she was being disloyal, and she crossed the room to look up at the little portrait of her mother. How to live in the house of a beautiful stepmother remained a puzzling and sometimes painful problem.

The family smoothly slipped into town habits and schedules that matched Pa's work in the newspaper office. Only Sarah Jane could not get used to the noises of Oshkosh. Louder than the country sounds of the farm, they were different from the city sounds she had known in Lincoln. They began early in the morning with the piercing whistles of the mills along the river, two steam sawmills, a shingle mill, and a window sash factory.

Jonathan laughed each time the mill whistles sounded, but Sarah Jane clapped her hands over her ears. "Why does Oshkosh have to be so noisy?" she asked.

"Better not complain!" her father told her one day. "Those mills are the lifeblood of this town. George Burnside was telling us yesterday that one hundred million feet of lumber were cut by those mills last year and one hundred million shingles. Don't you be complaining, daughter. I'd not have this good work if it weren't for those mills!"

One hundred million feet of lumber meant nothing at all to Sarah Jane, and after trying to count the shingles on Mrs. Patterson's house, at the front of the lot between their house and the street, and losing count each time, Sarah Jane decided that one hundred million shingles were too many to imagine.

As she helped her stepmother with the housework and the care of the baby, Sarah Jane often heard the school children running along the street to Mr. Raymond's Institute or to Mrs. Bryant's School for Girls on Algoma Street. A wave of homesickness swept over her for Miss Tillie Wallace and the room full of boys and girls in the yellow brick schoolhouse out near the farm. But Pa had explained with rows of figures on a sheet of paper how they could not afford the tuition fee for her to go to school until the house was paid for.

"Don't worry, Pa," she assured him. "I'll study and

read right here at home." And to herself she promised to get work as quickly as she could. Sadly she realized that a working girl would have neither time nor energy for school. But she could earn enough to pay the tuition fee for Jonathan so that he could grow up an educated man.

One cold stormy day, when Sarah Jane watched her father come tramping through the bad weather to eat his dinner, only to hurry out immediately afterward into the storm, she suggested to Rebecca, "why can't we cook his dinner and I'll carry it to him."

"A good idea," Rebecca agreed.

Each day when the mill whistles at noon announced the dinner hour Sarah Jane bundled herself in the heaviest shawl because a penetrating wind often blew up the Fox River from icebound Lake Winnebago. She carried a bowl of soup or a plate of stew or heated applesauce and thick sandwiches down Ferry Street to the newspaper office near the river.

She decided that it was not just the mills that made Oshkosh noisy. People—bustling, talkative, and argumentative—added to the confusion of sound. School boys going home to dinner from Mr. Raymond's Institute filled the air with shouts and snowballs. Girls skipping arm-in-arm home from Mrs. Bryant's school made Sarah Jane feel shy as she listened to their chatter.

As she passed the ironsmith's shop there was the re-echoing clang of metal struck against metal. Across the frozen ruts, on the west side of the street, the blacksmith would be shoeing a horse or mending some small tool or a wagon wheel. A volume of sound rolled out from the smithy: the blows of the hammer and the wheeze

161

of the bellows.

Beyond the blacksmith was a tavern. Sarah Jane walked swiftly past, afraid a man boisterous and happy with drink might stumble out and try to talk with her. In front of Smith's Corner Store, where High Street came into Ferry Street, men always gathered, talking loudly. No matter how the wind howled up the street they stood for a moment, unwilling to leave their argument.

Sarah Jane listened to their talk and wondered how long it would be before she felt a comfortable part of this noisy, busy town. By keeping her ears open she learned much of the news before Mr. Burnside printed it in the Democrat.

One group of men on a Friday argued about the newest song at Mr. Lake's Singing School at the Methodist Episcopal Church, up Ferry Street beyond Mrs. Patterson's house. That was where the Horner family went on Sunday mornings to sing and pray and listen to the rousing sermon by the pastor, Jabez Brooke. On Sunday evenings, while Sarah Jane put Jonathan to bed and watched over sleeping Charity, Pa and Rebecca went together to the Welsh church west of Ferry Street.

Sarah Jane walked very slowly as she listened to the men arguing about the newest song Mr. Lake had taught them at the singing school. Each sang a snatch of his own version.

Thinking of the beauty of her stepmother's voice, Sarah Jane felt it a pity that Rebecca could not go each week to the singing school. But members of the school had to pay a fee to Mr. Lake and buy the songbook.

And Sarah Jane, remembering her father's sheet of figures, realized that the pay which could not reach as far as school tuition for her could certainly not pay for singing school for her sweet-voiced stepmother.

Another day, sunny but cold, as she took Pa's lunch down the street, the men outside Smith's Corner Store were arguing about how long the sunny days would last. No one gave the same interpretation to weather signs. Each opinion was heatedly defended.

For a week Sarah Jane heard long, loud arguments about whether Mr. Potter could possibly have the plank road finished to Rosendale, thirty miles away, before snow flew next winter. Listening, she remembered the plank road from Sheboygan to Fond du Lac and the miserable miles she traveled over it after she had learned about her stepmother.

Another day, she walked as slowly as she could to hear every word of an argument about whether women should be allowed to belong to Mr. Raymond's Subscription Library. One dollar per year! If only they'd let women belong, she'd buy a membership for herself with her first spare dollar—as soon as she found work. Why shouldn't women belong to the library? she wondered. Women could read better than a lot of men.

There was discussion, too, outside Smith's store about whether the county should lend money to the railroad company to get rails laid to Oshkosh from the south. Listening, Sarah Jane remembered the locomotive named Winnebago on the lakeshore at Sheboygan. How excited Jonathan would be if the railroad trains came into town. It would be easier, too, for her to travel on her way if she could not find work in Oshkosh.

Going away seemed harder with each smile baby Charity gave her. But Sarah Jane was still resolved to honor her own mother in her own way, which meant being independent of her stepmother. She felt Rebecca's very kindness a threat because it tempted her to forget her mother.

In her daydreams, Sarah Jane imagined herself finding work in Oshkosh. Then she could be a part of all the exciting new things people were always talking about. And often at the end of the day she could visit Pa's home. She'd bring a toy and a pretty dress for Charity and a book or warm mittens for Jonathan. She sighed with pleasure at the picture she'd made of the future, but her feet hurried her toward the newspaper office before Pa's stew cooled too much to be tasty.

Mr. Burnside usually sat at his desk in the news-paper office, chewing a pencil and puffing clouds of cigar smoke into the air. The more trouble he had with his writing, the more smoke there was.

Sarah Jane preferred at first to avoid Mr. Burnside. He liked to tease her and she would blush before him and the two apprentice boys. But one day she brought doughnuts for everyone, and another day she mentioned hearing the men on the street talking about a city charter for Oshkosh.

"You've a nose for news, young lady, you have indeed!" Mr. Burnside exclaimed and clapped his hat on and set out to check up on the scheme.

When Pa was alone, Sarah Jane liked it best. The boys would be away running errands, and Mr. Burnside off about a handbill. Pa propped his feet before the potbellied stove in the center of the room. He ate his dinner while she busied herself in small ways around the shop. She'd pour coffee from the graniteware pot always simmering on the stove. Sometimes she'd find the broom and sweep the floor or perhaps she'd help with folding and wrapping the papers to be mailed.

One day Mr. Burnside caught her with broom in hand and teased, "First time I ever saw a female printer's devil, and a pretty one, too!"

When Sarah Jane looked shocked, the editor laughed at her discomfort and explained an apprentice was always a printer's devil. And she wasn't to be offended if she heard of a hellbox either. Broken type was tossed in there.

If they had the shop to themselves, Pa would eat and explain his work at the press, the typecases, and the composing stone. The mechanics of the press were no mystery to him. When something went wrong, as it frequently did, he soon found the trouble and repaired the damage.

Printer's ink sent out an acrid odor, a bookish smell, Sarah Jane thought. Even though she wrinkled her nose against it she liked it. This was Edward Horner's new world and it was responsible for his new lightheartedness, Sarah Jane knew.

Learning to set type seemed to come naturally to Edward Horner. But he had had very little schooling in England. Sarah Jane watched him at the typecase, finishing some copy after eating his dinner. He showed Sarah Jane how to read the type which he held upside down so that he could work from left to right across the type line. Sarah Jane read what he held.

"Look, Pa," she exclaimed, "*Officer* needs two f's."

Pa made the correction quickly, but his face was serious. Sarah Jane thought perhaps she had offended him. Children were not to correct their parents, she knew.

"I'm sorry, Pa," she said.

"Now, now," her father said. "It's all right, you helped me. Be glad you found the error. If it had got through, there'd be trouble. The editor of the Commonwealth published down in Fond du Lac likes nothing more than to catch a mistake in our paper. He'd publish it for everyone to read that the Oshkosh True Democrat doesn't know how to spell. Mr. Burnside would raise hob with us all."

Pa remained at the typecase, stick in hand, for his dinner hour was finished. Sarah Jane lingered because it was fascinating to watch the newspaper grow. Pa talked in strange jerks and spurts of conversation as he chose the right letters, repeating each once to himself under his breath as he dropped it into place.

"Reading has never been hard for me," he said. "But spelling . . . that's the hardest part of doing Mr. Burnside's job well . . . O-s-k-o-s-h—No, no! Have to be careful not to leave out that first h in Oshkosh—O-s-h-k-o-s-h—I never seem to get the hang of spelling—space, r-a-i-l-r-o-a-d—Did you know that your mother taught me to read? Started helping me before we were married. Gave me harder and harder lessons, even when you were a little bitty thing. You probably don't remember—g-r-e-a-t, space, b-e-n-e-f-i-t, space, t-o, space, O-s-h-k-o-s-h—Nights after I came home from the mill she taught me."

He put down his work and looked at Sarah Jane with a faraway smile. "It's not often, Sairy, that a man's blessed by two such wives as I've had."

Sarah Jane thought as she listened that perhaps she had been unfair to accuse Pa of disloyalty to her own mother. She wanted to talk with Pa longer, but the whistles were blowing the end of the noon hour. The two apprentices came noisily up the steps and into the Democrat office.

Hurriedly gathering up the soup bowl, Sarah Jane wrapped the shawl securely around her shoulders. With a wave to Pa, she went home.

17 *Payday*

WINTER BLUSTERED back and forth across Oshkosh all during March. Days of deceptively mild sunshine were sandwiched between days when the wind howled, wet snow piled up, and the robins who had appeared with the sunshine shivered wretchedly through the storms.

April brought many gray days with downpours of rain. Flocks of great geese winged overhead, and even through the wind Sarah Jane could hear the bugling sound of their call above the clouds. When the wind buffeted too fiercely, the geese sometimes landed on the shores of the lake to rest, feed, and wait for calmer weather. Sarah Jane walked to the lake to watch the geese and marvel at their strength and beauty and wild wisdom.

With May came starry crisp nights full of frog sounds, and sunny warm gardening days. Rebecca and Jonathan planted rows of vegetables and herbs, and along the house and bordering the edge of the yard, rows of flower seeds. In the warm twilight, Pa paced the little yard and talked of painting the house white.

With growing things and strong wings beating north, with changes talked of and planned for, and with water flowing strong and free toward its eventual meeting with the sea after a season prisoned in ice, Sarah Jane was alive and eager to answer an inner prodding. It was time for her, too, to be off and away, to honor the memory of Jane Horner.

The impatience and brooding resentment she had once felt toward her stepmother were no longer the motives for her action. Honesty made Sarah Jane admit that Rebecca was not a person anyone could hate— Rebecca with her household skills, her cheery laughter and beautiful songs, her wisdom with little ones, and her great loving patience with all of them.

No, Sarah Jane no longer resented her father's marriage to Rebecca. After a winter in this demanding, often cruel, country Sarah Jane understood that a man needed his wife. And a man like Pa especially, for he was so likely to "fly off at sixes and sevens" as Grandmum in England used to say when frustrations pressed him.

But still the memory of Jane Horner must not disappear, and keeping this part of the past alive was Sarah Jane's duty as she saw it. And so when she was inclined to relax in the happy life her stepmother built for the family an inner urging reminded Sarah Jane to make plans for the time when Rebecca no longer needed a girl's help.

How to begin might have been a difficult problem had not George Burnside unknowingly provided part of the solution.

One spring evening Mr. Burnside with his jokes and big cigar clomped into the little house to pay Edward Horner his wages for the winter months when money had been tight.

After Pa's coins had been counted out on the table,

Mr. Burnside turned to Sarah Jane. Lifting her hand, he put a five-dollar gold piece in her palm and gently closed her fingers over it. He laughed at Sarah Jane's startled eyes as she looked from his face to the coin in her hand.

"It's hard to put a money value on the tasks you've done around the Democrat office. No, no, don't protest! I've got eyes in my head, and maybe this little shiner will help you buy some heart's desire."

His laughter filled the room. Sarah Jane, truly speechless with surprise, could only curtsy a thank-you. The openhanded generosity of Americans was a trait she still found astonishing.

Another surprise was in store. Mr. Burnside turned to discuss with Edward Horner his plan to have him take the horse and rig next day to go to the Welsh community to collect newspaper subscription payments.

Sarah Jane sat looking at the gold coin. Her spirits soared. Then she shivered—this must be the answer to her indecision. Mr. Burnside's money would pay her way while she sought work by which she could earn her own living.

Suddenly Mr. Burnside's conversation was directed toward Sarah Jane again. His big voice brought her back to the present with a start.

"Of course Miss Sarah Jane will stay here and keep the home fires burning and do the ironing so that Mrs. Horner can ride along. Won't you now? Say yes, there's a good girl."

"Yes, yes of course," Sarah Jane stammered. "Yes, it will be nice for her to have a chance to see Uncle Thomas and his family and all the friends."

While Mr. Burnside gave Edward Horner directions for getting the horse and rig early in the morning Sarah Jane looked again at the coin in her hand. How swiftly things were happening! No time now to think of how much she'd miss all her stepmother did for the family, how she'd miss Jonathan and the rituals they had worked out through the lonely years in England, no time to regret being gone as Charity changed from baby to little girl.

When Pa and Rebecca came back into the room after telling Mr. Burnside good-bye, Sarah Jane asked without any preliminary explanation, "How much does it cost to go to Sheboygan?"

"Don't rightly recollect," Pa answered amiably, his mind still on the pleasant prospect of driving with his wife around the south end of the county, renewing friendships he had made during his first years in Wisconsin. "Planning on a trip soon, daughter?"

"Yes!" she exclaimed. She knew her father spoke jokingly, but the more she thought about it the more certain she was that she must heed the message of the gold coin. It was springtime, and with the birds and the floodwaters, she must be on her way.

"*You* are planning on a trip?" Pa asked, his voice now teasing. "Why don't you tell us the big news so that we can celebrate with you?"

Sarah Jane stood. Perhaps he would take her more seriously that way. She saw a startled, almost suspicious look grow in her stepmother's dark eyes. Rebecca shifted Charity to her shoulder and looked from father to daughter.

Then Sarah Jane plunged forward, her words coming

quickly. "I'm almost fourteen and I thought I could go to Sheboygan and maybe stop off first to see if Mrs. Wade would give me work at the inn. She thought I was a good worker last summer." She hesitated, knowing her plans seemed sudden. "I told you last summer, Pa, and I promised myself that I'd go as soon as I was not needed here—"

Recollection flooded back and Edward Horner re-lived that painful episode when Sarah Jane had so strongly rejected the news of a stepmother. "That was— that was when we were both upset," he said.

"I made my promise then," Sarah Jane said, trying to speak calmly. "And I'm not going back on my promise. All winter I've been trying and trying to think how I could earn enough to leave. Now Mr. Burnside's money will help me until I find work. And then—and then I'll help you with Jonathan—and Charity, too."

Angry glints began to gleam in her father's eyes. His face flushed, the color spreading from his collar up to the bald spot on his head. He spoke with a quiet voice that was frightening. "All winter, all winter, you've sat with us, meek and sweet, plotting to leave us! Why? Why!"

Sarah Jane's courage faltered. She put her hands on the table for support but she thrust her chin up and met her father's angry eyes. She was indeed at this moment truly her father's daughter in her determination.

"But Sairy, this is your home. I've given you a better home, humble though it is, than the one I was able to give you in England. Why ever in God's world do you want to leave when we've been a family again for such a short time in our own home?"

Here indeed was the hard question to answer. She did not know whether she could make her feelings clear to her father. And some of the difficulty lay in her own confusion. As the days passed, Rebecca seemed more and more a friend, the living person on whom Sarah Jane would like to pattern her ways. But she could never think of Rebecca as her mother. Jonathan now said "Mummy" and no longer "Mummy-Becky." It hurt his sister to hear him say it. Her loyalty and love to her mother's memory gave her strength to speak.

"I must go because this is your home and her home, and Jonathan and I are our mother's children. Oh! Mother must not be forgotten!"

Pa would have interrupted, but Sarah Jane had to finish.

"I hated Rebecca when you first told me about her— a stepmother to take my mother's place."

Had Rebecca looked angry, Sarah Jane thought, she might have been able to leave at that moment. Had she looked hurt or cried, Sarah Jane was afraid she herself would break into tears. But instead Rebecca's eyes were warm and waiting, her face calm in this crisis.

"I couldn't bear to have Jonny forget our mother. And here in this house it was Mummy-Becky, Mummy-Becky—and now just Mummy. He shouldn't forget our mother, Pa. Oh, Pa, it is so hard! I almost hated Rebecca!"

Sarah Jane covered her face with her hands and cried. Her father, deeply hurt and at the same time angry beyond words crossed the room and seized her shoulders.

He would have shaken her had not Rebecca cried out, "Edward, no!" The startling force of her words made him drop his hands and step back.

"She should have sense whipped into her," he muttered. "This talk of hating. She should be punished." He took a step again toward Sarah Jane, but again he was checked.

"Edward, does punishment heal hatred?"

The man shook his head, looking helplessly from his wife to his daughter.

Sarah Jane controlled her breathing enough to go on shakily, "At first I was going to take Jonny and go someplace where I could keep my mother's memory alive for him, too. But then I saw how good she is with him. He could eat and sleep and laugh and be a real little boy. I love Jonathan too much to take him away from her when she takes such good care of him. I tried—I tried all his life, but I couldn't. So I knew I had to go alone, for our mother's sake."

Her father shook his head before he said heavily, "I never heard such foolishness. Of course you took good care of Jonathan. You were only a child yourself—and you are still a child. Yet you talk of going as if it is yours to say when you go, when you stay."

His anger seemed to have drained away as rapidly as it had come. A kind of deep sorrow had replaced it.

Before Sarah Jane could say anything more Jonathan burst in the door. He was breathless and laughing. He and Jamie, Mrs. Patterson's grandson, had been playing tag in the twilight. He was unaware of the tension in the room. Chattering about tomorrow and the horse and buggy ride to see Uncle Thomas and Owen, he willingly let Rebecca put him to bed.

Sarah Jane had resumed her seat at the table and her father took a chair nearby. They sat quietly waiting for Rebecca to return. The room had grown dark except for the orange of the fire flickering through the cracks in the front of the cookstove.

Rebecca came back. She lit the lamp and drew her chair closer to the table before she spoke.

"I wonder," she said softly and slowly, "perhaps Edward, it is for her to say does she go or does she stay. She who when only a wee lass took a woman's burden."

Edward Horner cracked his knuckles in his distress and Sarah Jane shielded her eyes with her hand.

"Such hurt . . . such sadness . . . all because, Edward, she was not told about me. Shame upon me for not learning the words so I could have helped with the telling when it should have been done."

"The blame is not yours, Becky," Edward Horner said, reaching out to touch her hand. Sarah Jane nodded, agreeing with her father.

"Yes," Rebecca insisted firmly, "mine—and yours, Edward, too. There was too little telling, too little understanding."

The chunk in the firebox of the cookstove burned through and collapsed with a flare of light. Rebecca rose to replenish the fire.

Returning, she said, "Let us think and pray about this. Let us, Edward, you and I, take our trip tomorrow, collecting for the paper. Sarah Jane alone as she does the ironing can sort out her thoughts. No one pushes. If after thinking it through she still must go from my home to honor her mother, why then, our friends will help her find work. She'll go with our blessing, Edward. Yes, with our blessing, though our hearts will be heavy with the loss."

A silence, the kind of silence that comes when a storm suddenly abates, filled the room. Yes, tomorrow could take care of decisions. Now it was time to finish the evening tasks before an early bedtime.

 18 *Decision*

THE HORNER HOUSEHOLD, on other days so calm and well organized, was helter-skelter next morning. Rebecca was usually the quiet and orderly center around which the others revolved. This morning from the moment she lighted the lamp she flew about trying to remember everything and prepare herself for the day's expedition. She hummed happily and her eyes sparkled in anticipation.

At last Pa, looking his best after Rebecca's pressing and brushing, started down the street to the livery stable to get George Burnside's horse and rig. Jonathan, hopping up and down in his excitement, got in everyone's way. Sarah Jane put him out on the big stepping-stone before the door to watch for Pa.

"Don't you get muddy," she warned him, "or you'll have to stay home with me."

The lunch hamper was packed, Charity was bundled in shawl and bonnet. She cried loudly when Rebecca placed her on the big bed.

"Oh, tush hush," her mother scolded good-naturedly. "How can I pin on my bonnet with such noise in my ears?" She put the squirming baby in Sarah Jane's arms and went to the mirror to anchor her bonnet on her coronet of black braids.

"This is the way the baby rides!" Sarah Jane chanted, rocking back and forth from heel to toe to quiet the baby's impatience. Her reward was a gurgling, cooing laugh and a reminder that she'd miss her little sister if she reached the decision over her solitary ironing that she must keep last summer's vow to leave.

Just then Jonathan called from the door, "Look at Pa! Look at Pa! Here he comes. Quick, quick!"

Sarah Jane and her stepmother hurried to the door. As if he owned them and had been driving them all his life, Pa reined the spirited little black horse, Bess, up the narrow lane and stopped the handsome carriage beside the mounting block.

With his well-brushed hat hiding his bald head and excitement bringing a boyish smile to his face, Pa looked like the young man Sarah Jane had been searching for on the dock at Sheboygan last summer.

Climbing carefully over the wheel to keep his suit clean, Pa reached for Jonathan and swung him into the back seat of the carriage. Then he gallantly helped Rebecca into the front seat and settled the lap robe across her knees.

Jonathan leaned over his stepmother's shoulder, smiling and excited about the day's drive.

I wish it could be our own mother, sitting so beautifully in the carriage, Sarah Jane thought, but we had so little in England that there wasn't even a borrowed carriage for her to ride in. Sarah Jane blinked her eyes against tears.

Her stepmother saw. "Oh, poor Sarah Jane! You should be coming, too. Quick now, shake out the sprinkled clothes and climb in with Jonathan."

"Yes, come too, come too, Sar' Jane," Jonathan begged.

But Sarah Jane shook her head. "I have the work to do and I need to think. I like to iron. I'll be all right . . . You have a nice time. Tell Eliza and Miss Wallace hello for me. And Jonny, you give Uncle Thomas an extra hug for me."

Sarah Jane turned to see why it was taking Pa so long to climb into the carriage. He was taking something from his wallet, something small, wrapped for protection in a piece of cloth. As he unwrapped it, there was a golden glint in the morning sun.

"Daughter," he said, his voice unfamiliar and hoarse. "You belong with us—for years to come. But your mamma—but Becky—says I've not any right to dictate to you. Whatever you decide to do—go out on your own or stay here—I want you to have this."

He placed a little circle of gold in her hand. It was a brooch, a slender ring of gold with a delicate design of leaves around the edge. A name was engraved in the center. Tilting it in the sun, Sarah Jane read: Charity J. Horner.

"What—what is this?" she asked, puzzled.

"It's your own mamma's. The brooch I gave her when we were married. She always wore it at her collar. But when I went away, she took it off and gave it to me. To remind me of her love, she said."

"But Mother's name—I thought Mother's name was

Jane," Sarah Jane said.

"Charity Jane was her full name. But I told her it was too big a name for such a slip of a woman. Janie's what we called her for everyday. But the marriage papers said Charity Jane, and so I had the pin engraved like that: Charity J. Horner."

Charity! Charity! Sarah Jane looked up at the baby cooing happily in Rebecca's arms.

"You want me to have this?" she asked, moving the brooch so that it sparkled in the sun.

"Of course, dear," Rebecca said.

"Wherever you feel you have to go," her father said, "wear it and prize it in memory of your mother."

He turned toward the carriage, then he thrust out his hand to Sarah Jane. "Good—good luck, daughter," he said, shaking her hand with such a firm grip that her fingers tingled. Then he quickly jumped into the carriage, clucked to the horse, and they were off.

Sarah Jane followed them to the street, to wave until they disappeared from sight below the little rise where Ferry Street sloped down to the river.

Carefully carrying the gold brooch which had been her mother's, Sarah Jane walked back to the house and the duties and decisions waiting for her. She looked around for a safe place to leave the brooch while she set up the ironing board. On the shelf beside her mother's picture and Mr. Burnside's five-dollar gold piece was the safest place in the room.

When the brooch was placed well back from the edge of the shelf, Sarah Jane took down the little portrait of her mother and carried it to the window.

"Jane Horner, Charity Jane Horner," she said softly as she studied the pretty face in the tintype. And then again, "Charity, Charity Horner."

If she had lived, she might some day have had a baby girl whom Pa would have named Charity. But instead, it was Rebecca Horner who had that baby girl, and though Pa would have named her Rebecca or Mary Ann or Bronwen, Rebecca had named her Charity.

Sarah Jane could hear her stepmother's voice again, heavily accented in her earnestness: "No, Edward, she is *Charity* . . . sweet Charity Horner. Jonathan's sister—and Sarah Jane's—must be named Charity."

Not knowing her mother's full name, Sarah Jane had not understood then. But she understood now as she stood alone and faced making the decision which would honor best the memory of her dead mother.

Again out of the past of that weary night at the end of harvesting, she heard her stepmother's voice, "Sarah Jane! Don't ever make her ashamed of you."

Sarah Jane closed her eyes, more ashamed of herself than she had ever been in her life. While she, Jane Horner's daughter, had behaved like a spoiled child, Rebecca by word and deed had been striving lovingly to honor Jane Horner—Charity Jane Horner—to keep her memory fresh and lovely in their home.

"Oh, I am so ashamed," she said aloud, and started at the sound of her voice in the quiet room. "You would be ashamed of me, too, wouldn't you, Mother? Maybe I can start over. I hope you'll never be ashamed of me again—you or Rebecca."

She tilted the picture of her mother, staring into the

face, yearning for an answer of forgiveness and reassurance. Her close scrutiny showed her what she had not noticed before. Centered on the white accenting the neckline of Charity Jane Horner's dress was a little circle, the gold brooch which Edward Horner had given her on her wedding day, the brooch which now was Sarah Jane's.

"When I have finished the ironing," Sarah Jane told herself and laughed, feeling foolish to be talking to herself in the quiet room. "When I finish and have supper started, I am going to put on my second-best dress because it has a white collar, and I'll wear Mother's pin."

Hurrying to make up the time she had lost, she returned the portrait of her mother to its place on the shelf. She stirred up the fire in the stove, adding another piece of wood. She pulled the irons forward to the hottest part of the stove. While they were heating, she laid the ironing board across the backs of two chairs. Then from the shed she brought the basket of ironing which Rebecca had sprinkled the evening before.

Ironing was Sarah Jane's favorite duty in the house. With moistened fingertip she made sure the heat of the flatiron was right. Then she ironed quickly, smoothing fabric and expertly squaring corners as Rebecca had taught her to do. Ironing always cleared her mind and made her feel at peace with the world. It was good to do while making an important decision. But for a while she pushed aside even the need to make that decision and gave herself up to the enjoyment of the ironing.

Jonathan's trousers she laid aside. One knee was almost worn through. Rebecca did better mending than Sarah Jane could do. Rebecca matched grain of fabric and took such tiny stitches that the patch was almost invisible.

"I must have her teach me how to mend well," Sarah Jane said dreamily. Then she caught her breath. If she made her decision to go, it was too late to learn more from her stepmother.

Carefully she ironed Rebecca's best red dress, the one which brought more color to Rebecca's bronzed cheeks and made her dark hair glow and her brown eyes sparkle. Sarah Jane's mind followed each movement of the iron. Delay! Delay the decision. She had all day to decide about going.

She folded sheets and deftly smoothed pillowcases. If only she could smooth out her life's problems as well as she smoothed the laundered clothes!

Now she knew she no longer wanted to leave this home. It was her home, and here her mother had been honored more deeply and beautifully than Sarah Jane had known how to do. But faced by her own selfish behavior she told herself, "You don't deserve to stay here in Rebecca's home, making her extra work, reminding her of how ugly you have been."

When the ironing was finished and the fresh things were put away, Sarah Jane set the ironing board back in its place behind the kitchen door. She tidied the room, and then with a cup of tea she sank down in her stepmother's rocking chair to rest.

Her shoulders were weary from the long hours of ironing. Her feet throbbed from standing. And there was a blister on her left hand. In her anger at herself for her unkindness to her stepmother, she had slammed the hot iron on Pa's shirt, burning the fingers which guided the shirt collar.

She shut her eyes, trying to forget aching shoulders, tired feet, throbbing hand. But her mind would not stop racing. It took her to the cold pain of that moonlit moment last July when she had heard Pa tell the Wades about his wife.

"But why didn't I trust Pa?" she cried aloud. She could find no answer to put in words, though she thought about the four years and more since he'd left for America. It had been hard to put aside her daydreams and accept Pa as he actually was with his failures as well as his charm.

The house was quiet and Sarah Jane closed her eyes, tired in body from the work she had done, tired in heart from the conflicting emotions she was experiencing. She must have slept for a while, for when she opened her eyes the sun was shining in the west windows. Soon Pa and Rebecca, Jonny and Charity, would be coming home.

She jumped up and stirred the fire. She drew toward the hot part of the stove the stew her stepmother had left simmering that morning. She set the table so that everything would be ready for supper when her family returned.

There was enough time left to go to her side of the curtained bedroom and change into her second best dress with its white collar. She brushed her hair so that it made a smooth frame around her face. Standing on tiptoe to see herself in the mirror beside her mother's picture, she fastened the gold brooch in the center of her white collar.

The late afternoon sun lighted the wall and shelf holding the portrait of Charity Jane Horner. The oval mirror reflected Sarah Jane Horner. The resemblance was so strong Sarah Jane gasped—the heartshaped face, the hair smooth and parted in the center, the white collar, and the very same pin.

In the empty house Sarah Jane exclaimed aloud, "Why! I do look like my mother. Jonny has her coloring, but I look like her!"

By giving Sarah Jane the gift of the gold brooch, that strong link with the past, Pa had shown his daughter an important truth.

With this sudden insight, warmth and happiness spread through Sarah Jane. Only the silent house heard her next words. "I don't have to go away to honor Mother's memory. I only need to be like her in spirit wherever I am."

Now Sarah Jane felt a lightness, a happiness she could not bear in the empty rooms. She wrapped a shawl around her shoulders and went outdoors. No one was in sight. The sun was setting and the wind though carrying spring scents was chilly.

She went indoors again and sat down in Rebecca's rocking chair to wait. She knew now that she did not want to leave her family. But doubt in a great wave swept over her. Did she deserve to stay? She cried by herself briefly in the peaceful twilight and then something reminded her that she had never experienced unkindness from Rebecca. There was no reason to expect it now. Her head rested on the back of the chair and she rocked slowly until carriage wheels grated in the street.

Quickly she lighted the lamp and went to open the door. Pa carried in Jonathan, sleeping soundly after the excitement of the long day. Charity, too, was asleep in her mother's arms. Tiptoeing, Sarah Jane held the lamp while Rebecca tucked Charity in the cradle and drew the quilt over Jonathan who had not stirred when Pa put him on his bed.

Pa came back from the livery stable. He paced the floor, frowning at Rebecca and Sarah Jane as they worked quietly together, dishing up the supper.

When grace was said, Pa hesitated, spoon poised over his bowl of stew. He looked questioningly at Sarah Jane.

Rebecca spoke calmly. "It was so good a day for us. Fifty dollars your father brings for Mr. Burnside. It was good to see our friends. They send love to you, Sarah Jane."

Sarah Jane nodded. She was having difficulty swallowing.

Pa laid down his spoon. "For you, daughter? Was it a good day, too?"

Sarah Jane swallowed the lump in her throat.

"I learned a lot today," she said slowly. "I learned how hateful I've been. And I know now that I don't deserve to stay in your home. I'll go if you think it is best, but I want you to know before I go, Rebecca, that I understand what you have done. I hate myself for how I've acted . . . I love you. I do! I love *you,* Rebecca—and I love my mother, too."

She put her head on the table and cried. Pa and Rebecca both bent over her.

"What happened?" Pa demanded.

"You, Sarah Jane. You were not hateful. You were hurt!" Rebecca said.

Sarah Jane dried her tears and sat up straight. "Pa,

you taught me so much when you gave me my mother's brooch." She hesitated. There were so many things to say, and it was hard to know how to start. "Until you gave it to me I did not know Mother's name was really Charity, and so I didn't understand how lovely and unselfish you were being when you named the baby Charity."

She reached her hand across the table toward her stepmother. Rebecca placed both hands over Sarah Jane's.

"I hate myself for being so rude and so mean to you."

"But Sarah Jane," interrupted Rebecca. "You were not mean nor rude. You were hurt—too hurt for too long."

"No! I was impudent, that's what Pa called me one time, and he was right." Sarah Jane rose from the table and went to the shelf and took from behind Charity Jane Horner's picture the five-dollar gold piece Mr. Burnside had given her. She returned to the table.

"I truly don't deserve to stay in your home after the way I have acted," she said, speaking rapidly to Rebecca, feeling she must say it all at once. "I'll ask Mr. Burnside or the pastor to help me find work somewhere. It will make me happy to help you and Pa. But now I want you, Rebecca, to have this, to get something you want. Then you can remember I love you, not as I love my mother, but as I love you for your very own self."

Rebecca pushed her chair from the table and rose. Shaking her head, she clenched her hands behind her, refusing to take the offered coin.

Sarah Jane continued to hold the coin toward her stepmother, repeating almost helplessly, "Because—because I love you, please take it."

187

Then with a smile Rebecca accepted the coin. "Because I love you, dear child, I'll take. And this, this is what I want to buy with it."

She paused and pressed her palm against her forehead in the gesture of bafflement Sarah Jane had seen so often in first weeks in Rebecca's home.

"Oh, if my words came easier!" she said. "To help you understand. What money cannot buy, already you have given me—your love. When I knew you were coming from England, oh, I was so glad. You are the same age as my Mary Ann. You were going to fill the emptiness in my arms I thought. But I could not talk to you in your own words. And you were too hurt to come into my ready arms. But now, I speak better, yes? You know I am ready—when you are."

She stopped and looked solemnly at the gold piece. "And with this I want what we could not afford. All your father earns must go to living and buying the house. What I want most—it is an education for you and Jonathan. Tomorrow we go to Mr. Raymond's Institute to pay for a term of schooling. What is left, we buy material for school dresses, so you go to school unashamed of your clothes."

"But I wanted it to be spent for something for *you*," Sarah Jane argued.

"Nothing—no *thing* do I want so much," Rebecca answered. "School for our children, and the chance as for little Jonathan, to be mummy to you, too."

The meaning of all this left Sarah Jane weak and almost giddy. She felt so light and happy she could have floated across the room. And at the same time she was suddenly hungry! What a funny, what a *good* world it was! She slipped into her chair and picked up her spoon. Nothing ever tasted better than that stew, no bread was ever more like cake. She looked up and smiled at her father and stepmother.

Patting her shoulder in understanding, Rebecca turned to clear the table. Then she set the sponge for tomorrow's bread.

Her father's response was slower. He said, "Today we are a family at last. One family. The Lord be praised!"

Whistling happily, he brought his cello from its corner. Soon he was tuning each string, then the solemn, moving melody filled the room. He played "Old Hundred" and Rebecca's rich voice blended with the cello.

"Praise God from whom all blessings flow,
Praise Him, all creatures here below!
Praise Him above, ye heavenly hosts,
Praise Father, Son, and Holy Ghost."

Now, with this indeed her home and freed of the need to run away, Sarah Jane found herself bubbling over with the desire to sing. The solemn words had special meaning for her and she did not care if her voice was tuneless and a monotone.

But there was magic in this night. Sarah Jane sang freely, and her voice was high and sweet and clear, as Jane Horner's had been. Rebecca heard, and still singing, she came and put her arm around Sarah Jane as they sang the Amen in harmony.

In the lamplight Rebecca saw the burn on Sarah Jane's hand. As the cello music continued, she brought ointment and a bandage. "Tomorrow, a big day 'twill be," she said softly. "Be off to bed, my child, and peace attend thee."

And Sarah Jane felt that peace did truly attend her as she crossed the room. The jealousy and uncertainty that had so long crowded her mind were gone. She stopped by the corner shelf and smiled at the tintype of Charity Jane Horner. Such happiness filled her that she could not contain it.

Running back into the lamplight, she stooped over her father as he bent over the cello and kissed the bald spot on top of his head. Then she ran to Rebecca, rose on her tiptoes, and kissed her on one cheek and then the other. She spoke softly and clearly, "Good night, Mummy dear."